www.alohalagoonmysteries.com

ALOHA LAGOON MYSTERIES

Ukulele Murder
Murder on the Aloha Express
Deadly Wipeout
Deadly Bubbles in the Wine
Mele Kalikimaka Murder
Death of the Big Kahuna
Ukulele Deadly
Bikinis & Bloodshed
Death of the Kona Man

BOOKS BY CATHERINE BRUNS

Aloha Lagoon Mysteries:
Death of the Big Kahuna
Death of the Kona Man

Cookies & Chance Mysteries:
Tastes Like Murder
Baked to Death
Burned to a Crisp
Frosted with Revenge
A Spot of Murder (short story in the Killer Beach Reads
collection)

Cindy York Mysteries:
Killer Transaction
Priced to Kill

DEATH OF THE KONA MAN

an Aloha Lagoon mystery

Catherine Bruns

ACKNOWLEDGEMENTS

Thank you to retired Troy police captain Terrance Buchanan for again sharing his wealth of information and never tiring of the questions I ask! Judy Melinek, MD, forensic pathologist, was gracious enough to provide much needed assistance in the medical field. Much love to beta readers Constance Atwater and Kathy Kennedy, who are always there to provide honest and necessary feedback. Special gratitude to Kim Davis and Amy Reger for sharing their delicious original recipes. Thank you to my wonderful husband, Frank, for always believing in me. Last but not least, heartfelt appreciation to publisher Gemma Halliday and her editorial staff for all that they do.

CHAPTER ONE

———

"Don't cry, Jo." I placed my hand on the girl's shoulder as she turned her face away, not wanting me to see her tears. "Please don't cry for me."

She wiped her eyes with the back of her hand. "I'm not crying for you, darling."

I stooped down in front of her until our gazes were level with one another. "It's no use, Rose. I know. Please don't tell— um, oh *crap!*"

I stomped my foot in frustration. "I don't believe this!" This was the third time in less than a week that I had botched the names. I should have said Jo instead of calling her by her actual name.

"Nice going." Rose Fields, the blonde starlet who portrayed my sister Jo March, smirked as she called out to the man in the audience. "Jeff, she did it again!"

Jeff Temple, director *of Little Women, the Musical* that we were rehearsing for, was seated in the front row, cross-legged, watching our scene play out in front of him. I swear he rolled his eyes at me before he leaned over to say something to his assistant, Gary Stewart, seated at his left. Jeff rose to his six-foot-two-inch height and slowly strode to the edge of the stage.

He was powerfully built, with dark hair in a buzz cut and hazel eyes. In his early forties, Jeff was a good-looking guy, and I'd heard rumors—mostly from my friend Tad, the assistant stage manager—that Rose had unsuccessfully tried to get him to go out with her. I wasn't sure if this was a ploy to butter him up, but it was possible that she really liked him.

Jeff's mouth was tight and drawn as he stared at me. A fantastic director, he could envision scenes in a remarkable way, but wasn't a very patient man. Then again, I'd never heard of any director that had a great deal of tolerance. It was only yesterday that he had shouted at all of us and declared that trained monkeys could have performed better. Hey, it was all part of the business.

"Carrie." His tone was serious as he pointed at Rose, who placed a hand over her giggling mouth. "Let's try this again. Which character is Rose portraying?"

I sighed heavily. "Jo."

"Very good." Jeff didn't even attempt to keep the annoyance out of his voice. "When you are on stage, she is no longer Rose and you are no longer Carrie. The basics of Acting 101 at work. Try to remember that tomorrow night, please. Which happens to be *opening* night. Oh, and did I mention that we're sold out?"

Yeah, only about five hundred times already.

Jeff's eyes met mine, and a slow grin spread across his face. Sure, he was annoyed, but it looked like he wasn't going to start screaming at me, much to my relief. I couldn't blame the man for being ticked off. There was no excuse for my calling the wrong name. Once yes, but three times?

He stepped onto the stage and checked his watch. "Okay, guys, that's enough for one day. Everyone out front, please."

The rest of the cast appeared from backstage and gathered around Jeff like he was the Pied Piper. My good friend Tad Emerson hurried over to me.

"Don't worry about it, love," he whispered in encouragement. "They say that if you botch the rehearsal, that means the actual performance will go smoothly."

Tad had been a godsend for me ever since I'd moved to Hawaii a few months ago. He was a flamboyant type of guy, with hair dyed the color of silver and green catlike eyes that refused to miss anything. He was a delivery person for Lovely Linens, which serviced the Loco Moco Café, the restaurant I worked at.

"I hope you're right," I said. "Time's running out."

Jeff cleared his throat and counted off heads before he continued speaking. "Thanks for accommodating me today with my last-minute request for an early rehearsal. I know that most of you have jobs, so it was quite an inconvenience. Tomorrow night, as we all know, is opening night, so please be here by six o'clock sharp *at the latest*. The same for Saturday and then by noon on Sunday for the matinee. Any questions?"

Gary raised a hand. Although Jeff was good at his job he was also very demanding and quite relentless, so much so that his former assistant had up and quit last week when Jeff repeatedly had sent him out for coffee. Gary was in his early twenties and a communications major at a local community college. His easygoing, mild-mannered attitude made him a perfect match for Jeff.

"I'm still missing bios for a few people," Gary announced. "The production staff needs them this afternoon, or you won't be in the program. It's as simple as that. Rose and Carrie, I hope you have them handy."

Rose nodded. "Sorry about that, Gary. Mine's backstage in my purse. I'll go grab it." She tossed her head and disappeared behind the curtain.

Puzzled, I stared at Gary. "I handed mine in over a week ago."

Gary shrugged his shoulders. "Molly must have misplaced it. Sorry, Carrie." He handed me a sheet of paper. "Can you fill out another one now?"

"Sure." I wasn't going to make a big deal about it. The staff was doing the best they could to accommodate us. Most of the proceeds from the ticket sales went to pay for costumes, stage equipment, and various other theater-related items. No one received a paid salary except for Jeff, of course, and Molly, his part-time secretary, whose pay was probably more dismal than mine as a server.

Molly already had her hands full with the program, costumes, and actors' attitudes, namely Rose's. Rose seemed to think that as the lead, she was entitled to more attention than the rest of us and always had something to complain about. My costume had arrived in a size smaller than I usually wore, and the gingham dress was so restricting that it felt like an actual corset. I had chosen not to say anything and instead, had given it to my friend Vivian, an excellent seamstress, to fix rather than bother Molly. Cripes, this was only a community theater, and we all needed to make some sacrifices.

Jeff clapped his hands together. "Okay, guys, enjoy the

rest of your day. By the way, I'm happy to announce that Saturday's performance is also sold out. Who knew that Louisa May Alcott was so popular in Hawaii?"

Everyone whooped and hollered while Tad placed his lips next to my ear. "I bet word has gotten out about Jeff's friend coming to town."

There had been a lot of gossip flying around regarding a Hollywood director who was coming to see our show. He was a good friend of Jeff's, but no one seemed to know exactly who he was or when the mystery man was destined to arrive. An extra weekend had been added to the performance schedule for his convenience. Of course, every actress in the show fantasized about this man whisking her away to Hollywood, but I tried to take a more realistic approach. The chances were probably one in a million at best that he would find his next starlet at the Hana Hou Theater in Kauai.

Tad followed me down the stairs into the empty audience as I shot off a quick text to my boyfriend. I sat down and started to complete my bio as he stretched out lazily in the seat beside me.

"Where are you off to now?"

I looked up from the form. "To the Loco Moco. I was originally scheduled for the morning shift, but they switched me to two o'clock until closing because of the last-minute rehearsal."

Tad dangled his car keys. "I'm on my way to work too. Need a lift, love?"

"Thanks, but I just texted Keanu. He's on his way."

"Ooh, the K-man's coming for his woman," Tad cooed. "So romantic. How long have you guys been dating? And when you tell him to jump, does he ask how high?"

"Stop." I laughed. "It's not like that at all, and you know it. He's working the same shift as me today. Since rehearsal ended a little early, we might even have time for a quick lunch before we head over to the Loco Moco."

"Or maybe a make-out session instead," Tad teased. "You two always look like a couple of lovesick puppies when you're together."

Even though Keanu and I had been dating for almost three months, my heart still gave a little jolt whenever his name was mentioned. The awkward part of this situation was that Keanu Church was technically my boss. His parents, Terry and Ava Church, had bought the Loco Moco Café after the former owner was murdered. This happened right after I'd started working at the restaurant—in fact, I had been the one to discover Hale Akamu's lifeless body. With all the employees under suspicion, Keanu and I had joined forces to find the killer. The experience had drawn us closer, and we'd been inseparable ever since.

I waved my hand at Tad. "Let me finish my bio. I can't think with you jabbering like that. Will I see you at the café later?"

Tad shook his head. "I dropped off linens this morning before rehearsal." He blew me a kiss. "Until tomorrow, Miss Beth March. Tell Rose—oops, I mean Keanu that I said hello."

"Wise guy." I grinned as he made his way down the aisle and out the rear of the theater. There wasn't much to list on my bio, except for a few parts I'd had in high school. I thanked Keanu for his support and put down my pen. Sadly, there was no one else to thank. Most people mentioned how grateful they were to their families, but I had none to speak of.

About four months ago, I had followed my then boyfriend Brad to Hawaii in an effort to save our floundering relationship and escape my miserable home life in Vermont. My mother had ignored me for most of my life, and my older sister, Penny, joined forces with her, thus making me feel like an intruder in my own home. My father left us when I was only four years old. I had no idea where he was now or if he was even alive, for that matter. Thankfully, I had Keanu, but there was still a hole in my heart that might never be filled.

Jeff and Gary were still up on stage talking. I walked over and waited politely for them to finish before I spoke.

Gary leaned down to take the paper from my hands. "Thanks. I promise it won't get lost this time."

"Good." I smiled. "I'm an actress, not a writer, so hopefully they'll give it a good edit too."

The door at the rear of the theater opened, and Jeff glanced over in its direction. A broad smile crossed his face as he jumped off the stage and strode quickly up the aisle. "I'll be damned. Howie, you're early!"

I saw Jeff shake hands with a man about his age. He had short reddish-brown hair, and wore horn-rimmed glasses over a thin, angular face. His inquisitive brown eyes scanned the inside of the theater with obvious satisfaction.

"Temple, the place looks great. How's everything on the financial front?"

Jeff wiggled his hand back and forth. "Ask me after this weekend. I still need some investors. Interested?"

"Maybe," Howie replied. "Let's have lunch tomorrow and discuss it. My treat."

They both chatted on while I continued to watch in fascination. Gary jumped off the stage and came to stand next to me. "Do you know who that is?"

I shook my head. "No idea."

"Howard Livingston," Gary's voice sounded star-struck. "He's a Hollywood director and an old buddy of Jeff's. Jeff knew he was flying in today, which is why he upped the time for the dress rehearsal."

My jaw almost hit the floor. "*He's* the one? I mean, the one that—" I didn't want to mention the rumor, but Gary must have known the director's impending arrival was all that the cast had talked about for weeks.

He nodded. "Yep. He's the one everybody's been having fits about." He gave me a slight nudge forward. "Why don't you go do your 'It's no use, Rose' line for him and see what he says?"

Cripes, no one would let this go. "Real nice, Gary."

Howard glanced over at us curiously, and Jeff turned to see what he was staring at. He then gestured toward Gary. "Come on. I'll introduce you to my assistant."

Butterflies danced in my stomach as they came closer. Howard looked right at me and smiled pleasantly. *Oh my God.*

"Gary Stewart, this is Howard Livingston," Jeff announced. "Or perhaps I should say, the *one and only* Howard Livingston."

Gary extended his hand. "It's a real honor, sir."

Howie clasped Gary's hand in his. "Call me Howie. Everyone does." His gaze traveled back to me. "Is this lovely lady your girlfriend?"

Gary turned about ten different shades of red. "No, sir. This is Carrie Jorgenson. She's one of the actresses in *Little Women*."

Howie examined my face with interest. It wasn't a creepy nature—more typical of a man who enjoyed people watching for a living. He reached for my hand. "Miss Jo March, I presume?"

I flushed with pride. "No, I'm playing Beth. It's nice to meet you, sir."

He nodded. "The role suits you. Delicate, pretty. Jo's a tomboy, not as easy on the eyes, like you. I'm looking forward to your performance, Miss Jorgenson."

My heart pounded away so loudly in my chest that I was positive he could hear. "Thank you so much."

Howie nudged Jeff. "You'll never guess who I sat next to on the plane. No, wait. Let me put it another way. You will never guess whose *voice* I had to endure all the way from California. Six hours of pure torture."

Jeff frowned. "We know a lot of people who would fit that bill."

I laughed out loud at the remark, and they both stared at me. *Oops. Nice move, Care.*

Howie blew out an exasperated sigh. "It was the one and only Cremshaw. I swear I thought I might go deaf."

"You've got to be kidding." Jeff shook his head. "What the hell is he doing here? He was just in town a few months ago."

Howie shrugged. "Besides annoying us, you mean? It seems that Mr. Cremshaw refuses to leave paradise for long. Plus, there's rumors he's about to divorce his wife. If I know good old Randy, he's here to try to ruin someone else's restaurant and livelihood."

Jeff's expression was grim. "Well, I feel sorry for the next poor bastard he's about to descend upon."

"What does he do?" I asked with interest and then too late, remembered the conversation didn't concern me. Embarrassed, I covered my mouth. "Sorry, that's none of my business."

Howie grinned. "I like inquisitive actors. Randolph

Cremshaw—I call him Randy, by the way, because he hates the name—is one of the most renowned food critics in the world. You're probably too young to remember the movie critics Siskel and Ebert?"

"I've heard of them," I admitted.

Howie checked an incoming message on his phone before he continued. "Our buddy Randy is to food what those two were to movies. People think his word is God. Even worse? Randy thinks he's God."

"Sounds like a great guy," Gary mumbled.

"Where's he staying?" Jeff wanted to know. "Please tell me not in Kauai."

Howie placed his phone back in his pocket and gave Jeff a thumbs-up. "You win the pool. As a matter of fact, he's at the same resort as me—Aloha Lagoon. I must have done something bad in a previous life to deserve this."

Holy cow. Aloha Lagoon was where I worked. "Oh wow. I work in one of their restaurants. I hope he won't be dropping by." Poncho, our chef, would literally have a cow. Okay, perhaps pig was a more appropriate term, but either way, the visit was certain to cause some stress.

Jeff snickered. "The Loco Moco has been around for a long time, Carrie. Chances are he's already tortured them with his presence."

The back door of the theater opened again, and my boyfriend, Keanu, stood in the doorway. When he caught sight of me, he waved but made no move to approach us. I assumed he didn't want to interrupt our conversation, but I beckoned for him to come forward anyway.

Jeff raised a hand in greeting. "Hey, Keanu. How's it going?"

"Never better." Keanu's eyes searched mine.

My cheeks grew hot. "Mr. Livingston, this is my boyfriend, Keanu Church. Keanu, Mr. Livingston is a director from Hollywood."

I had told Keanu about the rumors, of course, but to his credit, he acted casual as he shook the man's hand.

"It's very nice to meet you, Mr. Livingston."

"Call me Howie," he said. "Your girlfriend is very

charming."

Keanu smiled. "That she is."

I adjusted my purse over my shoulder. "Thanks for everything, Jeff. Bye, Gary. It was very nice meeting you, Mr. Livingston—er, Howie."

Howie gave a slight bow. "The pleasure is all mine, Carrie."

He had even remembered my name. Excitement flooded through me, and then I forced myself to do a reality check. Howie was a friend of Jeff's, and he was only here to see the show as a favor. Still, it was a thrill to meet a real Hollywood director. Maybe he'd even give me some pointers.

Keanu held the door open for me, and we strolled toward his car, hand in hand, with the brilliant Hawaiian sun beating down on us. It was another beautiful day in paradise, and thoughts of Jeff, the show, and even Howie faded from my brain as I gave my full attention to the handsome man beside me. Keanu pushed me gently up against the side of the car and devoured my mouth while I responded ardently. I stared into those crystal blue eyes the same color as the ocean and had never been so happy or complete in my life.

Keanu dropped his hands to my waist, drawing me closer, and continued with the kiss. His mouth was hotter than the inside of a volcano, and I was positive I might erupt at any second. He was like a drug of choice for me lately, an addiction that I couldn't get enough of.

After we broke apart, breathless, Keanu opened the passenger-side door of his Jeep for me. When he was seated, he reached for my hand and brushed his lips against it. Some days I still couldn't believe my good fortune.

Keanu winked at me as he started the engine. "Those big brown eyes look pretty serious today. What are you thinking about, sweetheart?"

He deserved to know the truth. "Oh, I was wondering how I'd ever gotten so lucky."

Keanu flashed that adorable dimple of his. "That's funny. I was just thinking the same thing myself."

CHAPTER TWO

———

After getting off to a bit of a rocky start in Hawaii, I marveled at how things had finally come together for me. Besides Keanu, I had my own little apartment, a cat I adored, and was self-sufficient. The bonus was that I even liked my job—well, most days, that was.

Soon after arriving in Kauai, I had discovered that Brad had been cheating on me and dumped him faster than a cold cup of coffee. On my second day of employment at the Loco Moco, Hale had been murdered. With all the employees under suspicion, I had taken it upon myself to find Hale's killer and would have lost my own life if it hadn't been for Keanu.

I watched him now with admiration. Dark sunglasses covered his luminous eyes, which I never got tired of looking at. His strong, defined jaw gave off the authoritative air of a man who knew what he wanted out of life. He drew his thin lips together into a smile then focused his attention back on the road. His silky black hair was slightly disheveled due to the top being down and made him look even sexier than usual.

I'd worn my long, dark brown hair in a single braid and wasn't too concerned about its appearance right now. It felt wonderful to have the gentle, warm breeze blowing around my face while the nearby scent of eucalyptus invaded my nostrils. Keanu liked my hair loose and around my shoulders, but when serving food, it wasn't practical or sanitary.

We didn't have time to stop for lunch, so we grabbed bagels and drinks on the way and ate them in the car. Keanu had been at the café for most of the morning and would remain there until closing with me. Lately he worked more hours than the rest of us did.

"Ready for a fun-filled day? One of the dishwashers is on the blink, Poncho's been complaining about the poor quality of pineapples, and Mom and Dad are supposed to be stopping by this afternoon to have a chat with me. Maybe I'll get fired," he quipped.

I flinched inwardly at the words "Mom and Dad." Keanu didn't have to worry about getting fired, of course, but if it hadn't been for him, I might have found myself on the chopping block long ago. Keanu's parents had bought the café from Hale's widow a few months before, and even though I'd met them several times, we didn't have much of a personal relationship to speak of.

In addition to the restaurant, Mr. and Mrs. Church owned a chain of supermarkets in the Pacific Southwest. Keanu had mentioned that there were problems with some of the stores, specifically ones situated in Phoenix and Tucson, which explained why his parents had made quite a few trips between Arizona and Hawaii as of late. We had been scheduled to have dinner with them last week for the first time, but they'd had to cancel at the last minute. Keanu had assured me it was a business issue and nothing to do with me. I believed him but still had that insecure feeling they didn't like me—especially Keanu's father, Terry.

"Lead the way, my knight in shining armor," I teased as we entered the café from the patio entrance. There was also an entrance from the kitchen and one off the lobby of the Aloha Lagoon Resort, which we hardly ever used.

The wicker tables on the outdoor patio were covered by large, raised bamboo umbrellas to shelter patrons in case of rain. They were filled to capacity. Vivian Banks, my good friend and fellow server, was running between tables, delivering drinks and taking orders. She caught sight of us and raised her hand in a quick greeting while her amber eyes signaled an unspoken plea for help.

"I need to rescue Viv," I said as Keanu opened the door to the café for me. The inside was almost as busy as the patio. I noticed Keanu surveying the place and knew how proud he was of the restaurant, which in turn made me happy for him. He'd worked hard these past few months as the new manager, and it showed. Keanu enjoyed the job and customers, although it must have been a bit overwhelming for him at times, especially with his father constantly breathing down his neck.

The Loco Moco was pristine, with gray tiled flooring and granite countertops, oak tables and chairs, and the long counter with individual padded seats that ran in front of the coffeepot machine, register, and the double doors with portholes that led to an even more impeccable kitchen, where we were headed now.

Poncho Suarez was in front of the massive ten-burner stove, preparing a batch of his famous pineapple salsa. In addition to the treat, there were several other pots and pans with flames going underneath them. Chefs were such wonderful multitaskers.

Poncho was married with two young sons and in some ways like a father figure to me as well. We'd had several heart-to-heart talks since I had first come to the island. Poncho's life had not always been easy, and he'd managed to overcome a lot of obstacles. In some ways, we were kindred spirits.

With a balding head, slim moustache, and a stomach that protruded underneath his white double-breasted chef's jacket like a small basketball, he didn't represent the most intimidating of figures. However, when things didn't go as planned in the kitchen, his temper steamed like kalua pork in an *imu*, which I had recently learned was an underground oven.

Poncho's voice escalated as he talked to the young waitress standing by his side. Coral Palu had only been with us for a few weeks. She nodded intently at whatever he had said to her, but as soon as she spotted Keanu, her eyes became glued on him, much to my annoyance.

"You go ahead and get ready," Keanu told me in a low voice. "I need to see what's going on here."

I hesitated before going into the small employee room adjacent to the kitchen. There were lockers for employees to keep their personal items, with cubbies above them that held aprons and Loco Moco T-shirts. A staircase against the wall led to an office upstairs, where Keanu spent most of the day. If we were swamped, he always came out to help.

After I tied an apron on, I returned to the kitchen, where

Keanu was talking quietly to Coral. Her expression was mournful as she nodded in response.

"You need to be more careful," Keanu cautioned. "Every day this week you've dropped a plate. Just take your time. If you need to make two trips to the table, that's perfectly okay."

Coral batted her long eyelashes at him. "So I'm not fired?"

Okay, this sounded awful, but I kind of hoped that she would be. It was no secret that this girl had been ogling my boyfriend since the day she'd started. She knew we were together—we had made no secret about that. Besides, the Loco Moco had a gossip mill the size of the ocean. To be honest, I wasn't fond of the girl. Coral couldn't manage two words to me without sounding sarcastic.

Poncho, who was standing near them, didn't wait for Keanu's response as he thrust a plate into Coral's hands. "This order is for table number 5."

"Got it," she said.

Poncho stirred salsa in one pan and pork rice in another while he gestured toward another plate. "This hamburger is also for table number 5."

Coral reached in front of him to grab it. She was taller than my five-foot-four-inch status, with a figure that might have been a size two at best. Coral was Polynesian and had sleek black hair that hung down her back, like a shining halo. It was about as long as mine, although my dark brown hair had a bit more wave to it. She wore hers in a braid too. Coral had slightly slanted dark eyes that gave her an exotic look and skin so pale that it was almost transparent.

Although tiny-waisted, Coral was well endowed in the chest and wore the skimpiest outfits she could get away with. Even though she'd been here less than a month, Keanu had already spoken to her on at least three different occasions about her wardrobe. As she leaned down in front of Poncho, her girls practically popped out of the tight low-cut T-shirt she was wearing.

Poncho's eyes widened as he stared at her assets and then turned his beet red face at Keanu. "I just remembered that we're out of mangos. Make sure you order some more."

Keanu frowned slightly as the girl gave him a superior grin and then started toward the double doors, both plates in hand.

"Coral."

She turned around and gave him a megawatt smile. "Yes, sir?"

He cleared his throat. "You're not wearing a Loco Moco T-shirt. When you have a free moment, go to the ladies' room and change into one."

She noticed me watching from across the room and narrowed her eyes. "Sure thing, Boss."

Keanu walked into the employees' room and motioned for me to follow. He ran a hand through his hair, an indication he was agitated.

"What's wrong?" I asked.

He blew out a sigh. "We got a complaint about Coral's service yesterday. The customer said she was very snippy with them. Have you noticed her doing that before?"

Only with me. I hesitated before answering. I didn't want to come across like I had anything against the girl. "Maybe."

He raised an eyebrow. "*Maybe?*"

"It's probably best that I don't get involved."

Keanu put his hands on my waist and drew me closer. "You know I value your opinion."

I placed my arms around his neck. "Bummer. I was hoping there were other things you valued as well."

His eyes twinkled. "Well, I do confess to being fond of your physical attributes as well."

"Any in particular?" I teased.

"I'll make you a list," Keanu whispered as he covered my mouth with his. I sighed in contentment and reached my hands up to run them through his luxurious soft hair.

Someone cleared their throat, and we broke apart. I giggled, assuming it was probably Poncho ready with some smart-mouth retort and turned, ready to face him. Instead I found myself staring into the eyes of Keanu's parents. They stood there motionless, watching us in uncomfortable silence.

Keanu didn't miss a beat. He refused to let go of me although I desperately tried to wriggle out of his grasp. "Hey,

Mom. Dad. What's up?"

Terry Church's dark eyes shifted from me to his son in obvious disbelief. On the few occasions we had spoken, the man was always short with me. He was attractive for an older man with sandy blond hair, a well-defined chin, and wiry-looking frame. Keanu had assured me that his father wasn't much of a conversationalist, but I didn't buy it. Whenever we crossed paths, he tried to avoid me.

"Keanu, we need to discuss a few things," Ava Church said hurriedly, as if she sensed disaster was about to strike. My boyfriend got his looks from his mother, especially the ocean blue eyes. His personality was more similar to hers too. Ava always acted polite to me, and we'd chatted a few times about our mutual love of theater. She was also very sociable with Vivian and the rest of the staff. Everyone seemed to like the woman, but she had never mentioned my relationship with her son though.

My cheeks burned, and I stared at Keanu uneasily. He winked in reassurance and kissed my hand. "I'll catch you in a little bit."

I hurried out of the back room, positive I could feel Terry's intense hazel eyes burning through my skin. I had no doubt that Keanu was going to get a tongue lashing from his parents about making out with the hired help in the back room. Ava and Terry were probably convinced that we went upstairs to fool around when they weren't here. I shuddered at the thought. I wanted his parents to like me, and this little escapade certainly hadn't helped.

As I started toward the main room of the café, Vivian came bursting through the double doors and almost ran right into me. She grabbed my arm and led me over to the stove, where Poncho was busy preparing sandwich wraps.

"Ohmigod!" Vivian's eyes were huge in her oval shaped face. "You'll never guess who's out there."

Still upset about the encounter with Keanu's parents, I wasn't sure that I cared. "Who?"

"Randolph Cremshaw."

It took a moment for the name to register with me, and then Poncho and I both gaped simultaneously. "The world-renowned food critic?" I asked.

Vivian seemed impressed. "Dang, girl, you've been doing your homework."

I shrugged. "Not really. I just happened to—"

Poncho cut in. "Where is he? Out on the patio?"

Vivian shook her head. "He just sat down at a table in Carrie's station. I recognized him immediately from a recent article in *Star Magazine*."

Great. This was all I needed today. I blew out a long, steady breath. "Well, I guess I'd better go see what he'd like to eat."

Poncho was already peering through the porthole in the door that led to the café. He must have spotted Randolph because he snickered. "Looks like the man does not spend enough time in the sun."

"He used to live in Hawaii," Vivian volunteered. "He comes back several times a year to visit. And he always stays at the Aloha Lagoon when he comes to Kauai."

"Did he ever review the Loco Moco before?" I asked.

"I don't know," Vivian said.

Poncho did a palms-up and went back to the stove. "Not while I have been here. I doubt he is here to review, *ho'aloha.* Food critics like him specialize in restaurants that have fine dining, such as Starlight on the Lagoon." He pointed at the door with his spatula. "Nevertheless, do not keep the man waiting. And do not let on that you know who he is."

"Why?" I asked, confused.

He shook his head in fury. "No more questions. Go!"

Yikes. My fingers shook as I pushed my way through the doors. *Don't screw this up, Care.* Sure, he was only here to eat, but maybe he'd give the place a plug on social media if it met with his satisfaction.

I handed Randolph a menu and placed silverware on the table in front of him. "Welcome to the Loco Moco Café. What can I get you to drink?"

He looked up from the iPhone he was busy typing a message into—was he already taking notes on the place?—and gave me a quick once-over. "Coffee and water. I'm in a hurry and already know what I want. Bring me your signature dish, plus an order of home fries and toast."

I nodded and scribbled away on my pad. "So I guess by 'signature dish' you mean the Loco Moco?"

"Very perceptive, aren't you?"

His voice was thick with sarcasm, and for the second time in five minutes, my cheeks were on fire. Cripes, this man was rude. When he picked up his phone again, I took a moment to study him. Even though he was sitting, I could tell from the long gangly legs that he was tall, over six feet and about thirty pounds overweight. I surmised it came with the job.

The buttons on the Hawaiian shirt Randolph sported were stretched tight across the material and threatened to pop open at any second. He wore glasses with thick lenses and had a head of rusted colored brown hair with a receding scalp. Randolph's dark beady eyes reminded me of a rodent's, and he had a thick nose with wide nostrils above slightly crooked front teeth. His complexion was so pale that he seemed more suited for Alaska's climate than Hawaii's. A well-worn straw hat was placed on the chair next to his, as if echoing my thoughts.

Randolph looked up suddenly and frowned when he spotted me watching him. "Um, could I have my meal *today*?"

"Yes, sir." I hesitated because hash browns were considered a breakfast item, and technically we stopped serving the meal at eleven. It was after two in the afternoon, so I'd have to check with Poncho to see what he wanted to do. I tried to squelch my nerves as I returned to the kitchen.

Poncho was cool as a cucumber while he assembled Randolph's order. If he'd been serving the President of the United States, I doubted his mannerism would have changed. That was part of what made him such a successful chef—nerves of steel. Poncho ran a tight ship in the kitchen and was a bit OCD about certain things, like employees messing around in his fridge. We all tried to accommodate him by staying out of his way unless he asked for our help.

As I grabbed a glass of water for Randolph, I was distinctly aware of the mumble of voices coming from overhead. I was dying to know what Keanu and his parents were talking about and prayed that the topic of their discussion was not me.

Once I returned to the café, I poured a cup of coffee for

Randolph from the machine behind the counter then placed both beverages in front of him. "Would you like creamer? Your meal should be out shortly."

Randolph looked up from the iPhone again, and I noticed he was typing something into the notes section application. He saw my eyes wander toward it and placed his hand protectively over the screen. Ignoring my earlier comment, he sniffed at the coffee cup and took a small sip. He immediately made a face and then placed the cup back down on the saucer. "What is this garbage?"

The restaurant had started to empty out some, and I hoped no one had heard him. "Black coffee, sir. It's what you ordered."

He grimaced and shook his head. "No, honey. I wanted *real* coffee, not this crap. Now bring me the only kind that should be allowed in the world."

"What kind is that?" I asked, confused.

He stared at me like I had pineapples growing out of my ears. "Wow, please don't tell me that you grew up here."

What did that have to do with anything? "I'm from Vermont. I just moved here a few months ago."

Randolph snickered in obvious contempt. "That figures. So you're an authentic woodchuck. Did you feast on tree bark as well? No wonder you think that this mud will pass for *kope*. Did you know that's Hawaiian for coffee? Of course you didn't. Go tell your so-called boss that this patron wants *real kope*, made with fresh ground Kona beans. That's a good little girl."

Okay, I tried to be easygoing and pleasant with the customers since it was part of my job, and usually managed to be successful, even when some were downright rude. But this guy made my blood boil. I detested obnoxious people who thought that they were better than everyone else. Randolph was in a class all by himself, no compliment intended.

I managed a half smile for him and then turned away before my face betrayed me. I returned to the kitchen, where Poncho had the Loco Moco and hash browns ready.

"He wants his coffee prepared with fresh ground Kona beans," I said. "I know we've done that before but—"

He muttered a swear word under his breath. "Viv, can

you prepare a cup in the espresso machine for the king, please?"
Vivian's eyes were as round as saucers. "His nickname *is* the Kona man." She spoke the words in a halting manner, as if talking about a sacred idol.

"How do you know so much about this guy?" Poncho demanded.

Vivian placed the beans in the espresso machine. "He's married to Belinda Davenport, the former fashion model. One of them is always being mentioned in *Star*. There are rumors that she's having an affair and he plans to divorce her."

Poncho looked out the portholes again. "I hope she found herself a live one this time. That man looks like a walking corpse."

I carefully made my way back out to the café with his order, my nerves tingling and starting to get the best of me. Keanu and his parents were still upstairs, and I had the customer from hell to wait on. Still, I was confident that Poncho's cuisine would win him over.

"Here we are." My voice was cheery as I placed the plates down in front of Randolph. "Your coffee will be out in just a minute. Can I get you anything else?"

Randolph picked up his knife and fork. "Ketchup, and more napkins."

"Right away." There should have been a bottle already on the table. Since it was my station, I wasn't sure who would have removed it, but there were some newly filled ones in the kitchen to use.

Another customer was waving at me, and I ran over to give them menus and table settings. More people had arrived on the patio, and I hurried back into the kitchen. "Where's Coral?"

Vivian shrugged her shoulders. "Beats me. She's never where you need her to be. That chick is more trouble than she's worth." She whispered in my ear. "Plus, she's got her eye on your man. That's pretty obvious."

No kidding. My teeth gnashed together, but I merely nodded, not wanting to think about Coral and her tight T-shirts anymore. I reached out and grabbed a ketchup dispenser that was sitting near the stove.

"Who are you taking that to?" Poncho wanted to know.

"Mr. Cremshaw asked for ketchup."

"I'll bring it out with his coffee," Vivian volunteered. "I want to see him for myself. The man is a *legend*."

With great effort, I managed not to roll my eyes at her. "Be my guest."

Poncho and I watched through the portholes as Vivian dropped off the ketchup and coffee and made small talk with the food critic for a minute. Randolph's gaze traveled appreciatively down Vivian's lithe figure, and then his beady eyes followed her as she went out on the patio to take an order. *Ick.*

"Well, at least he seems to like Viv." I wondered how I'd managed to offend the man. We stared in fascination as Randolph dumped ketchup liberally all over his order of Loco Moco and hash browns.

Poncho uttered a moan low in his throat and covered his eyes with one hand. "I cannot stand this. I just cooked food for a man who has the eating habits of Homer Simpson. How is this joker one of the most feared and popular food critics in the world? How can he even attempt to taste the labors of my efforts now?"

Before I could reply, Randolph suddenly dropped the utensils and reached for his glass of water, downing it all in one gulp. Alarmed, I grabbed a nearby water pitcher and rushed over, Poncho at my heels. Randolph's face had gone from its sickly pallor to a bright cherry red.

"More water," he croaked and didn't wait for me to pour him some. He grabbed the pitcher from my hands and started guzzling directly from it.

Poncho's expression was horrified. "Sir, what is wrong with your food?"

Randolph banged the pitcher on the table so hard that we both jumped. He wiped his mouth with the back of his hand and stood, towering over my five-foot-four-inch height and glared at the both of us. "You think it's funny to treat a patron like this? Well, you're about to find out how funny it is."

"I do not understand," Poncho said. "What is wrong with the food?"

"Why don't you taste it and see for yourself. And don't forget to add lots of ketchup," Randolph taunted as he shoved his way past both of us and charged out the door that led to the lobby, slamming it hard behind him.

"What was that all about?"

With panic, I recognized Terry's stern voice and turned around. Keanu and his parents were behind the front counter watching us. *Perfect timing.*

My mouth went dry. "The man said that there was something wrong with his food."

Poncho took a small bite from the Loco Moco and muttered a four-letter expletive under his breath. "This is not ketchup that he put on his food. It is Tabasco sauce."

"Who is he?" Keanu asked. "A guest at the resort? Maybe we can track him down and apologize for the mix-up."

"He just happens to be one of the most acclaimed food critics in the world." Poncho pinched his nose between his thumb and forefinger.

Terry's eyes almost popped out of his head. "Please don't tell me that was Randolph Cremshaw. I heard a rumor this morning that he was staying at the resort."

Poncho nodded, his black eyes large and ominous. "The one and only. We are toast, my friends."

CHAPTER THREE

———

On Saturday, I walked the familiar path to the Loco Moco from my apartment, with a feeling of euphoria that life could not possibly get any better. If I'd had a decent singing voice I might have been tempted to burst into a chorus of Julie Andrews "The Sound of Music." As it was, Poncho and Vivian had been begging me not to sing karaoke at the café on Saturday nights anymore.

Sunlight streaked across the blue hues of the sky above as I observed the nearby ocean, fascinated by the subtle waves that always seemed to beckon me. They were calm today, but I knew how looks could be deceiving. Keanu was teaching me to swim—not an easy task for him since I was an unwilling student. I had almost drowned twice during my lifetime and had a deep-rooted fear of water that he was trying to help me overcome. If not for him, I would not have survived the last episode a few months ago when I'd come face to face with Hale's killer on a nearby pier and fallen into the water.

The beach was crowded with people, most of whom were most likely guests of the Aloha Lagoon Resort. The warm breeze felt wonderful against my skin, and I would have loved the opportunity to curl up in a chaise lounge and experience the hot sun on my face. Unfortunately, there was no time to indulge in such luxuries now as I hurried off to work.

The restaurant crowd was almost nonexistent, and Vivian was putting together some table settings behind the front counter. She looked up as I entered from the patio entrance and winked. "How'd it go last night?"

I assumed she was talking about my role in *Little Women*. "Fabulous. Opening night couldn't have been better. I didn't mess up once, and we had a full house to boot."

"That's terrific," she said. "I'm coming next weekend, remember. So, did you and your man celebrate?"

"We went to Starlight by the Lagoon for a late dinner and didn't get back to my place until after one." I'd had a difficult time falling asleep afterward, probably a result of the adrenaline pouring through my veins. Even though I was still elated about the performance, exhaustion had begun to seep into my bones, and I was quickly losing steam. If the place remained dead maybe I could take off an hour or two early and get in a nap before tonight's performance.

Keanu hadn't come inside the apartment with me like he usually did after our dates. His father had asked him to sit in on a board of directors meeting at the resort this morning. A couple of times a year, Keanu's parents flew higher-ranked employees into town to discuss the financial status of the supermarket chain. The "big suits" was what Keanu called them. He'd also mentioned the other day that his parents were thinking about opening a supermarket in Kauai during the next year or so.

Ava and Terry were grooming their son to take over the business someday, and Keanu didn't seem to be jumping for joy over it. I knew he was happy managing the restaurant, but he'd developed a *wait and see* attitude. I tried to be supportive and not interfere, yet it seemed to me that they were placing a lot of responsibility on their son's shoulders without asking what he wanted.

"And?" Vivian whispered. "Did you—um, do anything else?"

Good grief. If there was one thing I had learned about Vivian in the past few months, she was not the most subtle of creatures. Next to Keanu, she was my closet friend on the island. I was fond of her, but didn't kiss and tell. She'd been asking me the same question for weeks. Having grown up with a neglectful mother and a sister who didn't want me in their lives, I'd never felt the need to confide in anyone before. It was difficult for me to trust people, but I was slowly getting there.

"I told you before—we're not rushing anything," I said.

She gave a small toss of her short blonde hair. "You guys have been dating for what, close to three months? What's really going on here? Is it because of what happened with Brad? I know he messed with your head, but I honestly don't think Keanu would do that to you."

While living in Vermont, I had jumped into a physical relationship with Brad right after we'd started dating. I had told Keanu that I wanted to take my time, and he'd never tried to force me into anything.

"We'll know when it's the right time."

I didn't want to admit it to Vivian, but the issue was with me and me alone. There had been several times—especially in the last few weeks—when Keanu and I had come close to being intimate, but I always managed to hold back for some reason. We hadn't said those three little words to each other yet, but I felt them every time I looked into his eyes. For some odd reason, they refused to tumble out of my mouth though.

Vivian shrugged. "Well, be careful. Lots of girls are hot for him, in case you hadn't noticed, especially one in particular that we have the misfortune to work with. Coral is definitely an *I put out on the first date* kind of girl."

"Cripes, Viv. That's a nasty thing to say about anyone."

She wrinkled her nose. "Come on. Coral makes it so obvious. I mean, she practically drools every time he walks by her." Her face softened. "You're so lucky to have a guy like Keanu. Some days I wonder if all the good men are already taken."

"I used to wonder that myself. You're going to find a great guy too—I'm sure of it." My heart flip-flopped at the very thought of Keanu. "So is it just you and me this morning?"

She nodded. "Coral and Sybil are closing tonight. Coral is really starting to drive me nuts. All of her screw-ups just make more work for the rest of us."

I glanced around at the nearly empty restaurant. "Where is everyone?" There were only two tables of people out on the patio and one customer sitting inside. The beach was jam packed, so why was no one coming to eat here?

"It's so quiet it's almost creepy," Vivian admitted.

At that moment, Poncho flung open the door from the kitchen, slamming it into the wall and startling us both. "I'll tell you what's wrong." His eyes were black as coal and smoking with anger.

Vivian and I jumped back in alarm, fearful of his sudden rage. "What's the matter?" I asked nervously, not sure that I wanted to know.

Poncho gestured for us to follow him into the kitchen. There was a laptop sitting on the stainless-steel countertop that belonged to him. He kept it handy in case he needed to look up a certain recipe. I examined his face. Being half-Mexican and Polynesian, his skin tone was naturally dark, but at this moment it resembled more of a fire engine red.

He gritted his teeth and pointed at the computer. "Look what that jerk Cremshaw put on his blog this morning about the Loco Moco."

"Oh no," Vivian whispered.

"What made you look at his site? Did someone tell you it was there?" I asked.

Poncho nodded. "A friend of Terry's follows the rodent on Twitter. Apparently, he is posting his comments all over social media. This could have an even worse effect than if he had reviewed it for that hot-shot magazine he contributes to."

Vivian and I started to read the article silently to ourselves. It was entitled, "You'd Have to Be Loco to Eat Here," by Randolph Cremshaw.

Okay, this was not going to end well.

As my faithful readers know, Hawaii was my home for several years. I enjoy the tropical climate and always stay at the elegant Aloha Lagoon Resort whenever I return to the beautiful island of Kauai. I don't typically review cafés, but a recent visit to the Loco Moco, which wears the name "loco" well, has forced my hand.

The history of this restaurant itself is an interesting one, to say the least. The place was originally owned by George Kama, who then sold it to Maya and Sampson Akamu. The couple was killed shortly afterward in a car accident, and their son Hale ran the place solo for about twenty years. Hale himself was murdered a couple of months ago, inside the actual restaurant. Now if that wasn't enough to make you never want to look at a plate of their pork hash again, this is what I have to say about my recent dining experience at the hole-in-the wall

establishment:
Pass. That's all.
Service—Three stars. The server was attractive and pleasant but totally inept. I have my doubts that she could manage to walk and chew gum at the same time.
Beverages—One star. When I am served coffee in the beautiful state of Hawaii, it should not be in the form of mud, but a beverage that consists of freshly ground Kona beans. Eventually I did receive the latter after complaint, but the experience was already ruined for me. A bitter disappointment— yes, pun intended.
Cleanliness—Two stars. The best I can say is that the table wasn't sticky, and the server was nice enough not to place her gum underneath it.
Quality of food—Zero stars. That moment when you ask for ketchup but receive Tabasco sauce instead…well, what else is there left to say, except that I left the place in burning anger. Yes, another pun for you.
Average these ratings together and you come up with 1 ½ stars, or in my opinion a complete failure, so don't waste your time and hard-earned money here. Look elsewhere.
Skip the Loco Moco Café. You'll thank me for it later.

Vivian covered her mouth with one hand as she finished reading, and I sucked in some air. This would no doubt be very damaging to the café. I silently fumed about the line that stated the server couldn't walk and chew gum at the same time. *Excuse me?* I never chewed gum while I was working. *What a jerk.*

"How are Terry and Ava taking this?" I wondered if Keanu knew as well.

Poncho pressed his lips together tightly. "Not well. You just missed the latest episode of Terry's screaming. I think Ava has managed to calm him down for the moment. The one thing they seem very curious about is how Tabasco sauce ended up in the ketchup holder." He glanced piteously at both of us.

"I didn't do it," Vivian said quickly.

I shook my head back. "I filled some the other day, but I'm positive it was ketchup." I distinctly remembered pouring the contents from the large container into the holders.

Poncho muttered something indistinguishable under his

breath. "Anna filled a few the other day as well. Terry just called his royal highness—Cremshaw. Would you believe the man had the gall to tell Terry that he might remove the post from his blog if we would deliver breakfast and dinner to his room today? I am in the process of placing the breakfast items on a rolling cart. Carrie, he asked that it be delivered by the girl with the soulful dark eyes who waited on him the other day."

A giant knot formed in the pit of my stomach. *Great.* Ava and Terry were probably upstairs right now throwing me under the bus for the ketchup incident. How I wished Keanu was here. I'd asked him what had happened after they'd found us kissing—nothing, he'd assured me, and left it at that.

"Lovely." What was up with this guy anyhow? He didn't like me but commented that I had soulful eyes? Was he a pervert in disguise? I didn't want to go to his room alone. "Do I really have to wait on that creep again? I thought that food critics weren't allowed to say such nasty things. Can't he be sued for slander because of the remarks he made about the Akamus?" Mercifully, he hadn't identified me by name.

Poncho did a palms-up. "Ava and Terry are only concerned with giving the man whatever he wants right now. He is a freelance food critic and contributes to the most popular cooking magazine in the world. In short, he gets away with murder, and there's nothing we can do about it."

Vivian snickered as she helped us load the food onto the cart. "I bet he's got more than a few people that would like to murder him."

Poncho snorted. "It is tempting, *ho'aloha.* Believe me."

I stared at the contents on the cart. "What did he order? It looks like one of everything."

"I assume he must have a dining companion," Poncho said. "The man is a skinflint and disgusting on so many levels. You should have heard Terry on the phone, kissing up to the jerk. It was pathetic. I would never stoop so low. He even apologized to Cremshaw for your behavior, Carrie."

An electric jolt shot through me. "*Me?* What did I do? I was pleasant to the man." And God knows it hadn't been easy.

He shrugged. "Who knows? He probably made something up to tell Terry."

Before Poncho could say anything further, we heard footsteps on the stairs. Terry strode past us and examined the food. "Is everything ready to go, Poncho?"

Poncho nodded. "Carrie will take the food over now."

Terry turned and glared at me, his eyes menacing. "You roll the cart into the suite and then you leave. Do not say anything else to the man except 'Enjoy your food.' No small talk. Understand? Tell him to leave the cart in the hallway when he is finished. This is crucial to our restaurant, so if you'd like to keep working here, please do as I say."

His words stung like an angry wasp. I swallowed hard, afraid to say something I'd regret later. Why did this man dislike me so much? Because I was dating his son?

"Certainly."

He grunted something unintelligible and then stormed back up the stairs. Vivian and Poncho both stared at me with open mouths. Yes, the man could render a room speechless.

Poncho scratched his head thoughtfully. "Gee, I hope he comes around before the wedding. That would make family dinners awkward."

"Very funny." I picked up the order page, which had the room number printed on it. "Well, excuse me, but it's *Hi ho, hi ho, off to serve I go.*"

I wheeled the cart out into the lobby and rang for the elevator. I debated briefly if I should tell Keanu about his father's attitude and then decided against it. I didn't want to cause a rift between him and his parents.

I boarded the elevator, pressed floor 3, and exhaled a shaky, deep breath. Keanu was downstairs in the main conference room. I didn't know how long the meeting would last but hoped he would be back at the café before long.

On the third floor, I went past the grouping of rattan furniture by the elevator and pushed the cart down the hall toward suite 303. I knocked on the door, and it was immediately opened by Mr. Arrogance himself.

Randolph stepped back so that I could roll the cart inside. He was dressed in a dingy white undershirt and black slacks that dragged on the floor, his long, narrow bare feet poking out from underneath. I tried hard not to stare at the crusted-over toenails that screamed fungus at me.

"Welcome to my parlor, said the spider to the fly."

Yikes. For some reason, the word *icky* popped into my head. "Please enjoy your breakfast, sir. You can place the cart in the hallway when you're done, and one of our staff will pick it up later."

I began to walk away, and he grabbed me by the wrist. "Not so fast."

Startled by his action, I shook myself loose. "Don't touch me again."

"Sorry." Randolph gave a small smirk that said he was anything but sorry. He looked me up and down. "I'd like you to wait a moment until I'm sure the meal is to my liking."

I had news for this man—no meal was *ever* going to be to his liking. He lifted the covers off the plates one by one, examining the food while he grunted in apparent satisfaction. Finally, he picked up the white coffee carafe, poured himself a cup, and sniffed. Like the other day at the café, he took a small sip, grimaced, then shook his head at me. "Not quite, doll."

"Sir?" I was confused. Poncho had used his precious Kona beans this time, so what could be the problem?

"It's cold. Bring me another carafe right away."

I couldn't believe my ears. Anger bubbled at the surface and threatened to boil over any second. What I really wanted to do was throw the entire carafe in his face, but then I'd be out of a job and, knowing Randolph, looking at a lawsuit.

"Is there a problem, dear?"

The man clearly enjoyed the fact that he was goading me, but I was determined not to let him get under my skin. "No, sir. I'll be back in a few minutes."

"Text Chef Paunch ahead of time," Randolph taunted, "so that the coffee will be ready when you get back. That's a good little girl."

I bit into my lower lip to temper my reply. "His name is *Poncho.*"

"Whatever. He's got quite the paunch on him, so my name fits. And do hurry up. I haven't got all day." He sat down and started to eat, dismissing me with a wave of his hand.

Could the man be any more pretentious? I counted to ten

and compressed my lips together, afraid a nasty comment might slip out between them. As I started toward the door, I spotted two half-filled mimosa glasses sitting on the table on the balcony. I wondered if good old Randy might have had a girl over last night—or perhaps his estranged wife had joined him.

"Are you deaf?" Randolph bellowed. "I want my coffee—*now*!"

With great effort, I opened the door to the suite and managed to refrain from slamming it behind me. On my way back down the hallway toward the elevator, I grabbed my phone out of my jeans pocket. My fingers flew as I texted Vivian.

Tell Poncho that the jerk said the coffee's not hot enough. Have a new carafe ready to go when I get back. It's a wonder no one has killed this guy yet.

When I arrived back at the restaurant, the coffee wasn't quite ready, so I waited by the entrance in the lobby until Vivian brought it out. I didn't want Terry to see me. This carafe was so hot that the heat radiated through it, despite the potholder she'd wrapped around the handle so I wouldn't burn myself.

"Try not to throw it in his face," Vivian cautioned, as if she could read my thoughts. "Do you want me to take it over for you instead?"

"No thanks. If I don't come back, Randolph will know he's gotten to me, and I won't feed his ego. Is Keanu back yet?" Sometimes he stopped back over at the café if there was a lunch break during the meeting.

She grinned and shook her head. "No, I haven't seen lover boy. Why don't you text him?"

"I doubt Keanu would stare at his phone during a meeting. He's not the type. Oh well, since we're slow, maybe I'll treat myself to a little walk on the way back and soak up a little of the Hawaiian sun while I have a chance."

"Meet Carrie Jorgenson, who always finds the positive in a totally crappy situation," Vivian teased. "Good luck."

I hurried back toward the lobby and the elevator. I managed to make it back to his room in less than fifteen minutes. *I will not insult the man. I will not insult the man.* This would hopefully be the last time I ever had to lay eyes on Randolph Cremshaw again. Like Vivian said, I always did try to seek the good in a bad situation.

As I knocked on suite 303, I noticed that the door was slightly ajar. I waited for a response, not wanting to enter and, with my luck, see the man naked this time. *Ew.* That was a sight that would surely have haunted me forever. At that moment I heard a weird gasping type of sound and pushed the door open. "Mr. Cremshaw?"

When I stared at the sight before me, my hands flew to my face and the coffee carafe went crashing to the floor. The pain didn't even register as the hot liquid rose upward and spewed all over my bare arms.

Randolph was lying on his back on the plush, carpeted floor. His entire body convulsed as he thrashed around, unable to speak. He clutched at his throat, and there was foam coming out of his mouth. The expression on his face was pure terror as he looked at me. His mouth opened wide, and he emitted a long, continuous wheezing sound.

"Ohmigod!" I screamed and knelt beside him on the floor. He must have had some type of attack. Maybe he was diabetic? Shaking almost as badly as Randolph, I reached into my jeans pocket for my phone and dialed 9-1-1. The call was answered immediately.

"9-1-1, what is your emergency?" A brisk female voice asked.

"Please help." I struggled to keep my voice calm. "I'm in suite 303 of the Aloha Lagoon Resort with a man who's having breathing problems."

"Is he choking, ma'am? Do you know CPR?"

I stared down at Randolph. "Are you choking?"

The wheezing noise had stopped and Randolph was still, his open but unseeing eyes focused on the ceiling. A chill rolled through my body as I reached out to check his pulse.

"Oh God." I whimpered like a frightened child.

"Is he conscious, ma'am?" The operator wanted to know. "Can he speak at all?"

Terror enveloped me as realization quickly set in. This couldn't be happening. *No. Not again. Please, no.*

"Ma'am?" The operator spoke again. "I asked if the man was conscious."

I rested Randolph's hand gently on the carpet and whispered into the phone. "No. He's dead."

CHAPTER FOUR

"Well, well. We meet again, Miss Jorgenson."

At the sound of the familiar voice, my body stiffened. I glanced up from the floor where I was sitting outside of Randolph's suite. An EMT was attending to my burned arms while another technician and a police officer were inside the room with Randolph's body, presumably waiting for the coroner to arrive.

"Hello, Detective Ray." My voice sounded hoarse.

Detective Ray Kahoalani and I had first become acquainted a few months ago when I'd found Hale's dead body one night after work. According to recent rumors, it seemed that Aloha Lagoon had a bit higher of a homicide rate than most towns in Hawaii. Still, I doubted that anyone on the island had the misfortune of finding as many dead bodies as me.

From what I knew of Detective Ray, he was a native islander. He had a round tanned face with dark hair that had started to turn gray at the ends. His intelligent brown eyes crinkled at the corners as he looked down at me with a sympathetic smile. As usual, he was dressed in his standard uniform that consisted of Hawaiian shirt and khaki trousers. I'd lost count of how many Hawaiian shirts the man owned, but this particular one was yellow with large blue flowers on it. Ray was one of those people who blended well into crowds with no outstanding characteristics. Perhaps that was why he chose to become a detective.

I didn't know Ray's exact age but speculated that he was in his late forties or so, probably close to Poncho's. The good detective was looking a bit haggard today. Perhaps those rumors of the island's shrinking population were true after all.

Detective Ray addressed the technician, who was busy placing a bandage on each of my upper arms. "How she's doing? Should she go to the hospital?"

The technician closed his medical bag and rose to his feet. "The lady certainly can if she wants, but I think she'll be fine. Fortunately, they're only first-degree burns." He smiled at me. "Would you like us to bring you over?"

I shook my head. "No, thank you. I'm supposed to perform in a show at the Hana Hou Theater tonight. There's no reason I can't, right?"

The EMT gave me a wry grin. "The show must go on, right? Is your costume long sleeved by chance?"

Thank goodness for circa 18th-century dresses. "Yes. I'm in *Little Women, the Musical*." There had been a lot of advertising for the show in the *Aloha Sun* newspaper recently, so I thought he might have heard about it.

"Oh yeah." The technician snapped his fingers. "Good luck. My girlfriend's going to see it with her sister next weekend. Just be careful. If the pain gets worse, make sure you call your doctor or go to the emergency room."

I thanked him and continued to sit there without moving, sensing what was coming next. My entire body was numb, and I wondered if I might be experiencing some degree of shock.

Detective Ray extended his hand to help me up then led me over to the rattan couch located near the elevator. "I need to ask you some questions, Miss Jorgenson, if you're feeling up to it."

I wasn't, but knew he'd ask anyway. "Of course."

The elevator pinged at that moment, and an attractive-looking woman started in the direction of Randolph's room then stopped when she saw Detective Ray. Rachel Wein was the assistant manager of the Aloha Lagoon Resort and a few years older than me. She had long chestnut hair and was very petite-like, even with the four-inch heels that adorned her tiny feet. I didn't know Rachel personally, but Keanu had introduced me to her once when she'd stopped by the café.

"Oh, Detective Ray, I just heard what happened." The woman hesitated when she saw me watching her then stared in confusion at my bandaged arms. "Is everything all right?"

Detective Ray gave a curt nod. "Rachel, do you know Carrie?"

I wasn't sure if she'd remember me, but her gaze traveled down my face to the coffee-stained Loco Moco T-shirt, which must have helped jar her memory. She smiled warmly. "Of course. You're one of the servers at the Loco Moco." Her eyes widened suddenly. "Did *you* find Mr. Cremshaw?"

I nodded mutely.

Rachel moved to stand beside me and took my trembling hand between both of her warm ones. "Is there anything I can do to help? Shall I call the Loco Moco for you?"

The thought of Terry running over here, red-faced and screaming while he asked how I had managed to kill Randolph, didn't hold much appeal. Yes, I needed to notify the café because they'd be wondering what had happened to me. Plus, Vivian was the only other server currently on duty. But there was someone else that I needed to see first—the one person I'd come to depend on in the last couple of months.

My throat was parched, and I longed for a glass of water. "Do you happen to know if the board of directors meeting for AKT Markets is still going on in the conference room downstairs?"

Rachel nodded. "Yes, they have the room reserved until five o'clock. Is there someone in there you'd like me to locate for you?"

A sense of renewed hope filled me. I had texted Keanu a few minutes ago, but he hadn't responded. I knew it had been a long shot. He would give the meeting and its speakers his full attention and probably not even look at his phone during the entire session. "Yes, please. My boyfriend, Keanu Church, is in that meeting. Would you mind asking him to come up?"

"Oh, of course." Rachel flashed me a genuine smile, and I instantly warmed to her. "I know Keanu. I'll go find him right now."

"Thank you so much." Gratefully, I leaned back against the floral cushions and closed my eyes.

Detective Ray cleared his throat. "So you're dating Keanu now? You did seem quite chummy the last time I saw you both together. It was right after he'd saved your life, I believe."

"Yes, we're very chummy these days." My tone sounded snarky, but I didn't really care. I'd been here and done this all before—the entire questioning routine. My arms ached from the burns, and all I wanted was for Keanu to hold me in his muscular ones and tell me that everything would be okay.

"Don't his parents own the Loco Moco now? The restaurant you're employed at?" Detective Ray made notes on his pad.

What was he getting at? "Yes." I hoped Ray wasn't about to offer us dating advice. There was always *Cosmopolitan* if I was really desperate.

"So, this makes body number two for you, Miss Jorgenson. You seem to have a knack for stumbling upon them."

That was the understatement of the year. What was it with this island and dead bodies anyhow? I definitely wasn't feeling the aloha spirit.

"How about we start with you telling me what you were doing delivering food to Mr. Cremshaw?" Detective Ray asked. "Last I knew, the Loco Moco didn't provide room service."

I placed my hands in my lap and stared down at them. "Mr. Cremshaw is—was—a food critic. He came to the restaurant on Thursday, but not to review." I debated about how much to tell the detective, then realized how incriminating this all looked for the Loco Moco, and me. "He—uh, had a bad experience and said some unpleasant things about the restaurant on his blog."

Detective Ray jotted down some notes while I cursed my ability to always be in the wrong place at the wrong time.

"Did Mr. and Mrs. Church ask you to bring food over to try to make amends?" he asked.

"Something like that." The man was relentless in his questioning.

"Did Mr. Cremshaw say he would revise the blog if you provided a meal? Or was he looking for something else?"

Like what? "I don't understand."

Thankfully, the elevator dinged again and Keanu emerged. My heart leapt and surged with pride when I noticed how handsome he looked in a lightweight navy fabric suit that brought out the magnificent color of his eyes. I had never seen him dressed up before. Of course, he looked great in anything, but...*Oh for crying out loud. Focus, Carrie. Focus. You just saw a man die.*

Keanu's worried gaze met mine, and he rushed over to us. "Carrie!" Ignoring the suit, he dropped to one knee in front of me as his expensive Italian black loafers scraped across the rug. If he'd proposed at that moment, it would have been very difficult for me to say no.

His gaze traveled down to the bandages on my arms. "What the hell happened? Who hurt you?"

I caressed his cheek with my fingers and smiled. "It's fine. I got burned with some hot coffee, that's all. Sound familiar?"

On my second day of employment at the Loco Moco, I had accidentally spilled hot coffee all over Keanu's arm. He'd been a great sport about it, and the episode had become a standing joke between the two of us, but he wasn't laughing now.

A muscle ticked in Keanu's jaw, and his voice was stern. "I asked who hurt you."

Detective Ray reached his hand across me to shake Keanu's. "Nice to see you again, Mr. Church."

Keanu cut his eyes to the detective, as if seeing him for the very first time. "Hello, Ray. Can someone please tell me what's going on here?"

I squeezed his hand in earnest. "I brought a cart of food over here for Mr. Cremshaw. He complained that the coffee wasn't hot enough, so I went back to the Loco Moco to get him another carafe. When I returned, he was lying on the floor, having convulsions." I stopped to try to collect my bearings as the unpleasant vision rolled through my head again. "He died while I called 9-1-1."

Keanu muttered an expletive under his breath. "I can't believe this is happening to you again!"

Yeah, join the club. "When I saw him lying on the floor, I guess I dropped the carafe, and some of the coffee spilled on my arms. I really don't even remember it happening."

Detective Ray jotted more notes down on his pad. "So the door to the room was unlocked the second time you came back?"

I nodded. "I knocked once and heard a weird noise, so I pushed it open. That's when I saw Mr. Cremshaw lying on the floor."

The detective tapped his pencil against his teeth in a thoughtful manner. "Any chance there could have been something wrong with the food?"

The color rose in Keanu's face. "What exactly are you suggesting, Detective?"

Detective Ray merely shrugged. "Maybe nothing. We have to wait for the autopsy to know for sure, but from what Carrie has told me, it sounds like Mr. Cremshaw could have eaten something that resulted in his death."

I knew Ray was testing us and didn't comment, but Keanu was visibly furious. He was always so laid back and mild mannered, but right now the vibrant blue of his eyes shot angry sparks at the detective, making my insides quake nervously.

When he finally spoke, his voice was low and steady. "Look. The man said some rotten things on his blog and Twitter about the Loco Moco, but we didn't kill him because of it. That would be insane."

Detective Ray ignored Keanu and addressed me. "Carrie, did you see anyone else in the room with Mr. Cremshaw either time or any signs that someone had been there?"

That was when I remembered the drinks. "There were two glasses of mimosa—they were each about half-full when I went in with the cart the first time. Maybe someone was in the bathroom. I've heard rumors that he and his wife were having problems."

Detective Ray's face was unreadable. "I'm not interested in rumors, just the facts. So, either someone had recently left the room or perhaps they were hiding in the bathroom when they heard you at the door, is that what you mean?"

"I guess." My voice was on edge, and I longed for the line of questioning to be over with so that I could go home. In desperation, I clung to Keanu, and he sandwiched my hand between both of his.

"It's okay, baby," he whispered, as if reading my mind.

A small Asian woman approached us from the direction of Randolph's room. I vaguely recalled her entering the suite with another policeman while I was having my arms bandaged. She had long, sleek black hair, delicate porcelain skin, and dark eyes that were both observant and sharp.

Detective Ray stood when the woman reached us and offered his hand. "Nice to see you, Dr. Yoshida."

She grinned. "Come on. Is it ever really nice to see *me*, Ray?"

They walked a few steps away from us and huddled together, talking. "That's Dr. Aimi Yoshida from the coroner's office," Keanu whispered. "One of the staff pointed her out to me a while back when she was investigating another death here at the resort."

Cripes. How many people had died here? Was this the Bates Motel in disguise?

I cocked an ear in their direction. Dr. Yoshida talked in a normal tone while Ray was obviously trying to keep things on the hush-hush so we didn't over hear them.

"You know I hate to comment without all the facts, but it appears this might have been some type of poisoning," Aimi said. "That would be in line with the convulsions and the foaming at the mouth Mr. Cremshaw suffered before he died. But we'll have to wait for the toxicology tests to know for certain. All of the food and beverages he consumed will be tested as well."

I glanced uneasily at Keanu, whose mouth was drawn tight and grim. We both knew that there was no way the food could have been poisoned. Vivian and Poncho were the only other ones who'd had access to the cart's contents, and I'd personally stake my life on their innocence.

"Good," Ray said. "Apparently the staff told me on my way upstairs that he was some type of celebrity, a renowned food critic."

Aimi nodded. "I see what you're getting at. Yes, that should allow me the luxury of putting a rush on things, but the toxicology tests will still take several days at best."

She shook hands with Ray and gave Keanu and myself both a little finger wave before she disappeared back down the hall in the direction of Randolph's suite.

"Detective." Keanu's tone was quiet but firm. "I'd like to

take Carrie home now. She's been hurt and needs to get some rest."

Despite the pain in my arms, I was okay, but didn't bother to contradict him. Keanu was beyond annoyed at the detective's implications, so it was better if we left as soon as possible.

Detective Ray picked up his pencil again. "Can I have both of your phone numbers in case I need to get in touch?"

Keanu rattled off our numbers, and Ray scribbled them down. "What about your parents, Keanu? Are they at the café now?"

"I believe so." Keanu looked at me. "Did you see them this morning before you left?"

And how. "Yes, your father and I spoke before he sent me over here."

Keanu narrowed his eyes. "My father sent you over? I don't like this. Why did he do that? It's not part of your job."

"It wasn't his fault," I added in haste. "Mr. Cremshaw asked for me specifically."

Detective Ray looked interested in this tidbit of information. "Mr. Cremshaw asked for *you*? Did he try anything while you were in the room alone with him?"

Keanu fumed in silence while I shook my head. "It was nothing like that. The man was rude and tried to annoy me. He complained that the coffee wasn't hot enough. I think he enjoyed the fact that he had us all groveling at his feet."

Keanu pursed his lips together, and there might have been actual steam pouring out of his ears as well. The entire episode wasn't painting his parents, me, or the Loco Moco in a very good light. Maybe I shouldn't have elaborated so. When would I learn to keep my big mouth shut?

Detective Ray put his pad away. "Was the review in the *Aloha Sun* today?"

"No," Keanu answered shortly. "Cremshaw had a popular food blog, and he also reviewed for *Dining Is Divine*. He told my father on the phone this morning that he might think about featuring his so-called review in there as well."

It appeared that Keanu had done his homework on Randolph too. I didn't know how much of a blog presence

Randolph had, but if it rivaled his other accounts, we were done for. After he'd left the restaurant on Thursday I'd checked him out on both Twitter and Facebook. The man tweeted about 50 times a day, and it was usually something negative. He had over two million followers on Twitter and roughly 800,000 likes on his Facebook page.

Keanu put an arm around my shoulders and led me toward the elevator. "Well, if that's all for now, Detective, we'll be on our way."

"By all means." Ray's gaze met mine, and the smile he radiated had the power to send icicles down my spine. "I look forward to seeing you both again very soon."

CHAPTER FIVE

Keanu gripped the steering wheel tightly between his hands. "I feel awful that I didn't see your text right away."

My arms burned as I drew the seat belt across my lap. "Don't worry about it. When you didn't answer, I asked Rachel to go find you."

"I'm glad you did." As we drove out of the parking lot and headed for my apartment, he navigated the steering wheel with his left hand and reached for mine with his right. "You're more important than some dull meeting, or anything else, for that matter."

He was the first person to ever tell me such a thing. My emotions were raw, and I struggled for composure but it was no use. I wiped away a tear that dripped off my chin.

"You mean so much to me too."

Keanu drew my hand to his mouth before the light changed green. "Don't cry, sweetheart. I'm sorry you had to go through this. And I don't want you going back to the café. You need some rest. When you stopped in the ladies' room, I sent my father a text and explained everything that happened."

"Keanu," I began. "The restaurant is short staffed as it is."

He shook his head. "No arguments, Carrie. You've been through an awful ordeal."

"How'd you know about Randolph's blog?" I asked.

"My father sent me a message earlier this morning, before I went into the meeting. He's very good at expressing himself."

"What does that mean?"

He gave a wry grin. "He used all caps and several

exclamation points. My guess is that he might have been acting a bit psycho at the café this morning."

I didn't answer.

Keanu blew out a sigh. "Frankly, I'm a little pissed off at my father for sending you over to the resort to grovel at that man's feet. The place was dead, so he should have sent Poncho. That wasn't your job."

"Well, Randolph did ask for me, so what was he supposed to do?" And why in God's name was I defending Keanu's father?

He flashed me a contrite look. "We didn't know anything about the guy, except that he's a public figure. What if he'd attacked you?"

"Please don't start anything with your father," I implored. "It will just make things worse."

He pulled his car up in front of my apartment building and stared at me, confused. "Make what worse? What are you talking about?"

Oh boy. This was uncomfortable for me to say. I didn't want to sound like a baby or put him at odds against his parents. "Your parents—well, at least your father—doesn't seem to like me very much."

His eyes widened in surprise. "Carrie, that isn't true. They just need to get to know you better. We'll have dinner with them soon."

Oh yeah, I was really looking forward to that event.

Keanu came around to help me out of the car and placed his arm around my waist as we walked toward the front door. I placed my key in the lock and hesitated. "Um—"

"What?" he asked. "Come on—out with it. We said we'd always be honest with each other."

I forced myself to look directly into his eyes. "Sometimes I feel like they think I'm not good enough for you."

His jaw dropped in amazement. "That's crazy. You're beautiful—inside and out—smart, warm, and kind. Everything that I desire."

My heart dissolved into a giant puddle at the words. Keanu was terrific for my ego. "Maybe my insecurities are working overtime."

Keanu put his hand over mine as I attempted to turn the knob. "Did my father say anything else to you?"

I didn't want to mention Terry's flare-up earlier. "He was fine."

"You're telling me the truth?"

I opened the door and pretended not to hear him. My apartment was on the first floor of a three-story brown stucco building. It was only an economy style, but I loved it anyway. There was a modest-sized kitchen, a small living room area, bathroom, and one bedroom. The entire space was only about 800 square feet, but size didn't matter. The overall effect was cozy and just right for me.

Benny, my orange and white cat, was waiting by the door for us expectantly. He glanced from me to Keanu and yawned, then meowed plaintively. When I picked him up, his paw hit one of my burn marks, and I winced in pain.

Keanu noticed my reaction and took Benny from me before I plopped down on the couch. "How's my buddy doing today?"

Benny meowed again in response, and Keanu scratched him behind his ears. I adored the fact that Keanu was an animal lover, and he'd regaled me with plenty of tales about the golden retriever he'd owned as a child. His current apartment building didn't allow pets, but he was looking around for another place—maybe even a house—where that would no longer be an issue.

Keanu's apartment was three times the size of mine, but he'd often commented that he preferred my place over his. I had recently bought a blue plaid couch with overstuffed pillows, a matching armchair, glass-topped coffee table, and an end table from a local secondhand store. The set worked well with the beige pile carpeting. In addition, I'd also bought an oak dresser and a new double bed with a mattress that was beyond comfortable. That was all I needed right now, besides, I couldn't afford anything else on my modest income. Keanu had offered to help financially many times, but I always refused.

Keanu knew that I didn't like to leave Benny alone for prolonged periods of time, another reason we spent more time at my place. Secretly, I was afraid that Terry or Ava might show up unannounced on their son's doorstep bright and early one morning and find me there. I had the distinct impression they thought we were sleeping together, even though that wasn't the case.

Keanu placed Benny on the floor and sat down next to me. He shrugged out of his suit coat, stripped his tie off, and pulled me into his arms. "Are you sure you're all right?"

Content, I rested my head against his muscular chest. "I'm okay, now that you're here."

He lifted my face between his hands, looked deeply into my eyes, and then brought his mouth down hard on top of mine. With a sigh, I placed my arms around his neck and closed my eyes. His lips, hair, the scent of his woodsy cologne—everything about the man was addicting. I wanted the kiss to go on forever.

In a couple of minutes, I'd rid Keanu of his oxford, and my stained Loco Moco shirt was lying on the floor next to it. He trailed a path of kisses down my neck and chest. His deft fingers were gentle on my arms, and he carefully avoided the bandages so as not to hurt me. Forget the burns. My entire body was on fire, and I might go up in flames at any moment.

Keanu's hands moved over my body and without meaning to, I stiffened. He sensed my hesitation right away and stopped kissing me, then drew back so that he could study my face. "Everything okay?"

I stared into his beautiful eyes, and my heart was instantly torn in two. Not knowing what to say or how to explain my behavior, I simply stared down at the floor. He exhaled a long, ragged breath and let go of me then reached for his shirt on the floor.

"Sorry," I whispered. "It's not what you think."

He spoke quietly. "Carrie, I'm *never* going to force you into something you're not ready for or that you don't want. But I have a feeling you're holding back for some other reason. Are you—" Keanu stopped, and his expression twisted into a frown. "Are you unsure about your feelings for me?"

"No!" Startled, I placed my arms around his neck. "Don't ever think that." *I'm the problem.*

He stroked my hair, his hands lingering on the strands for several seconds. "You're afraid that I might hurt you."

"I know you're not Brad. You really do care about me."

This was the part that didn't make any sense. My relationship with Brad had always been more on a physical level than emotional. I could discuss anything with Keanu. In fact, we'd had several all-night gab sessions in person and over the phone. We were good together, and he'd never given me any reason to think he might be like Brad. So what exactly was I doing?

"I'm crazy about you," Keanu said in a low husky voice, and pulled me onto his lap for another kiss. His hot breath on my face drove me close to distraction. "I'd be lying if I said I didn't want to be with you now—in the worst kind of way."

My entire body tingled at his words but I didn't reply. Besides Brad I'd only had one other serious boyfriend, who'd dumped me after graduation when he moved out west for college, taking a piece of my heart along with him. It was safe to say that my track record with men wasn't the greatest but I'd surmised from the beginning that Keanu was different from the rest. My brain knew this, but someone still needed to explain it to my heart.

"It's all right," Keanu kissed me again. "We have plenty of time."

Before I could respond, his phone pinged, and I moved off his lap so that he could answer it. His handsome face grew stern as he read the text.

"What's wrong?" I asked, suddenly fearful.

He glanced up from the phone, clearly distracted. "Dad's asked me to come to the Loco Moco right away. Detective Ray wants my parents down at the police station for questioning, and they would like me to be present as well."

It shouldn't have come as a surprise that Detective Ray would be interrogating the Churches. Terry had talked to Randolph shortly before he died, and the café's food was the last that he had eaten before his death. But to think that his parents had anything to do with the crime was ludicrous. We'd been down this road before—not Keanu's parents, but the rest of us Loco Moco employees—when Hale had been murdered. It was a journey I had no desire to travel again.

"Your parents depend on you a great deal." I couldn't resist saying the words out loud, because it was the truth. They seemed to be dumping a lot on him all at once, and Keanu wasn't one to complain. At twenty-six, Keanu had barely gotten his feet wet as manager of the Loco Moco, and now they wanted him involved with their supermarket chain too. I suspected he worried about letting them down.

He shrugged. "I have responsibilities that I can't ignore, Care."

My phone pinged with a text from Vivian. *So sorry about what happened! Are you okay?*

I texted back. *Better now, thanks.*

She responded immediately. *You left your purse here. Do you want me to drop it off at your apartment?*

No, I'll come grab it. Keanu will drive me.

Vivian's next response came within seconds. *No one expects you to come back to work. Sybil will be in early to cover. Coral went home sick. Like I really believe that one.*

Coral's antics were the last thing I was worried about. *Okay, see you soon.* "I'm going with you," I said to Keanu and went to the bedroom to grab a new shirt. "My purse is still at the Loco Moco."

"Why don't you stay here and rest before the show? I can bring it to you later."

"No, I'll wait there until you get back from the station. I'd rather not be alone right now."

He frowned. "I don't think I can make the show tonight. Today's events have put me behind, and I have checks to write for vendors and payroll to report."

"It's okay," I assured him. "Tad can give me a lift when it's time. You came to the performance last night anyway."

His expression was suddenly pained. "Some days I'm not sure if I want all of this."

Oh God. My heart constricted inside my chest. Maybe this was why I'd been careful about us becoming intimate so soon. Keanu wasn't ready for a serious commitment either. Now I felt foolish. "I'm sorry. You don't have to come to the show again. Seriously, most people only go once. It's fine, really."

"Hey." He lifted my chin with his hand. "I wasn't talking about you. If it was possible, I'd be at every performance." His blue eyes shone as they stared into mine. "I was so damn proud of you last night. Not that I'm not proud of you the rest of the time too, but you know what I mean." He paused, a small catch in his voice. "You played the part so well, you almost had me convinced you really were sick."

He must have been thinking about his sister, Kara, who had died years ago from cancer. She'd been his only sibling, and from the way he always spoke about her, it was obvious how much he'd adored her. Beth March, the character I portrayed in *Little Women*, was a frail girl who grew sickly from scarlet fever and never gained her strength back. She ended up dying at the end of the play. While eating up the praise, it hurt me to know how much my performance might have affected him on a personal level.

"You're thinking about Kara, aren't you?"

He didn't answer, but his sober expression told me that my assumption had been correct. I longed to kiss the pain away but instead, placed my arms around his waist. "She must have been a lovely person."

His voice was gruff as he kissed me. "It's been a long time. I should be over this by now."

"I don't think you'll ever get over it," I said honestly. And certainly his parents never would. Another thought occurred to me. "Is that why your Dad is—so—so distant?"

Keanu waited a moment before he answered. "Yeah. I figure on some level he's afraid to get too close to me because of it. Maybe he thinks he might end up losing me the same way. Kara was his little princess. Both my parents were devastated when she died, but he took it particularly hard."

"And now he's putting everything on you," I said.

My words sounded unpleasant, but Keanu smiled in understanding. "He means well, really he does. They're both worried about the blog post, and now Cremshaw's death could prove detrimental to the restaurant. Plus, there's more."

Of course there was. "What else?"

He raked an agitated hand through his hair. "The register has been coming up short the past couple of weeks. Altogether, the losses add up to a couple of thousand."

I sucked in some air. "Who do they think is responsible?" *Please don't say it's me.*

He tweaked my nose. "Don't go there, Carrie. You know

I would never suspect you, and neither would my parents."

Well, certainly not Keanu and maybe not Ava, but Terry probably thought I was capable of stealing a homeless man's shoes. "I want to believe that."

Benny hopped up on the arm of the couch and nudged Keanu with his paw. Keanu scratched him under the chin, and Benny's purrs were so loud that they threatened to drown out our conversation. "There's nothing for you to worry about, okay? My parents know how much you mean to me. My father will come around eventually."

Terry had asked me to make sure everything went smoothly this morning. I was not supposed to speak to Randolph—just provide impeccable service. Instead, the encounter had ended with Randolph dead. Something told me that Terry wasn't about to welcome me with open arms into his family.

"I'm sure you're right," I lied, and then locked the door behind us.

CHAPTER SIX

When we arrived at the restaurant, Keanu's parents were standing outside waiting for him. Terry's eyes narrowed when he spotted me sitting in the front seat of Keanu's car.

Yeah, nice to see you too.

Ava glanced from me to her son and then husband, almost as if she expected a tornado to strike at any second. Nevertheless, she smiled pleasantly as I emerged from the car. "Carrie, are you all right? How awful that must have been for you. Please don't feel like you must come back to work. Sybil's already here."

I was touched by her concern. "I'm okay, thanks, Ava. It was just a shock to my system."

"We'd better get going," Terry said curtly to his wife. "I don't think we should keep the police waiting. There are a lot of things we need to explain. What a coincidence. The same day Cremshaw's assault on the Loco Moco hits his blog, he's found dead after our hired help delivers food to him."

Oh yeah, he definitely couldn't stand me.

Keanu frowned at his father. "Carrie shouldn't have been there in the first place, Dad."

Terry pretended not to hear his son as he opened the passenger-side door for Ava. "Let's go."

"I'll drive myself," Keanu said.

"I was hoping you'd come with us," Terry said. "There are a few things I'd like to speak with you about on the way over." He cut his eyes to me again, and I was startled by how cold they were. I shivered inwardly. Even the hot Hawaiian sun couldn't warm me now.

"We'll have to do it later. I need to get gas anyway."

Keanu leaned down to kiss me, and I shrank backward in sudden panic.

"Not in front of your parents," I whispered.

He merely grinned and touched his lips against mine. "They need to get used to it. Good luck tonight, sweetheart. If you're gone before we get back, I'll pick you up after the show."

"Good luck to *you*." The Church family was going to need it as they went up against the inquisitive and sometimes irritating Detective Ray.

Keanu got into his Jeep, which was parked next to his parents' Mercedes. Terry gave me one last disapproving look before he got behind the wheel of his car, and they all drove away.

"I see that went well."

Vivian was standing behind me, purse slung over her shoulder. Her face was pale, but she managed a smile.

I exhaled noisily. "It's obvious that his parents adore me, isn't it? Jeez, Viv, you don't look so good."

"I'm going home," she said. "I've been lightheaded and nauseous all morning. I hope it's not that bug which has been going around. The place is dead anyway. Sybil's here, and Anna's coming in shortly as well. They'll both close tonight, so don't worry about anything." She stared in fascination at my arms. "Holy cow, are *you* all right? I can't believe you found Randolph dead. It's already all over Facebook that he died, and people know that the Loco Moco delivered food as some type of peace offering."

Cripes. "How did they find out?"

Vivian shrugged. "Someone at the resort must have squealed. People on social media are nicknaming us the Killer Café, Arsenic and Old Loco, you get the idea."

This was becoming a living nightmare. Okay, time to change the subject. "So Coral didn't seem sick to you?"

Vivian shook her head. "I really hope Keanu cans her butt. My guess is that she's the one who filled the dispensers with Tabasco sauce too."

I'd been thinking the same thing. "Why would you say that?"

Vivian looked at me in surprise. "Come on. She's so

freaking jealous of you it's pathetic. You should have seen her face when you and Keanu walked out of here the other day, holding hands. Mark my words—if she'd had a gun, she would have used it. I'll bet she was hoping you'd be blamed for the sauce because you were the last one to fill the dispensers."

"Why would she be jealous of me? That doesn't make sense."

"Gee, no idea," Vivian mocked. "You're a lovely person, the customers adore you, and oh yeah, she seriously wants your boyfriend. No reason at all for her to be envious."

I sighed. "Viv, you'd better go straight home to bed. You're getting delirious."

"Text me later, and let me know how the show went."

"I will. Feel better."

The inside of the Loco Moco was quiet. There were two couples sitting and conversing in low tones at separate tables. The sky was overcast and the patio was completely vacant.

Sybil was waiting on one of the tables. She was twenty, and went to the local community college. Vivian and I both got along well with her. She generally didn't want too many hours but had upped her workload during the last couple of months.

Sybil spotted me and gave a small wave. I returned the gesture and then went into the kitchen, where I found Poncho muttering to himself at the stove. He looked up at me, and then his eyes immediately wandered to my bandaged arms.

"Ho'aloha, I heard what happened. Are you okay?" The concern was evident in his voice.

"Yes, thanks." I exhaled sharply. "It was a shock and caused me to spill the carafe, which then burned my arms. The coroner thinks he might have died from some type of poisoning."

"The Kona man," Poncho murmured in a theatrical tone, more to himself than me. "What if the very drink he loved was the death of him?"

His words seriously creeped me out, and I watched as he removed a tray of pineapple cookies from the oven. "We don't know that the coffee was poisoned."

"But it would fit," Poncho insisted. "I just finished reading an article about him. The man was a caffeine junkie. Sometimes he would have as much as ten cups a day. And he loved his Kona coffee with a passion, which is how he got his nickname."

"*Ten* cups a day? No wonder he seemed so nervous and jittery."

Poncho snickered as he placed the cookies on a cooling rack. "I do not like to speak ill of the dead, but that man was a true *poho*."

I wrinkled my nose. "Do I even want to know what that means?"

He handed me a cookie. "Hawaiian slang. It means he was a waste of time. In my opinion, the man was a waste of precious air as well. What goes around, comes around. First off, a real food critic always pays for his meal, whether he likes it or not. And the fact that he bargained for free food with Terry is considered deplorable to the entire industry."

I took a bite from the cookie. It was still warm from the oven and moist, bursting with the juicy taste of fresh pineapple. "Oh, this is so good. But how come you're baking?" Poncho never had time to make desserts. We sent out for pies and cakes from a local bakery because he had all he could do just to manage the entrees some days.

"I will pack some up for you to take home," Poncho said. "I may have plenty of time for baking if business stays like this. Terry was acting like a lunatic this morning."

"I saw, remember?"

"Even before you came in," he continued. "He left a voicemail for Keanu when he couldn't reach him. He screamed so loud that the walls and the floor above me shook. Thank goodness we did not have customers at the time."

At that moment, I pitied my boyfriend. He hadn't mentioned the voicemail tirade, only that his father had sent several texts. Terry needed to take a lesson in patience from his son. "How long do you think Randolph's post could affect business for? Permanently?"

Poncho shrugged. "Hard to say. It might not have been so bad if Cremshaw had not up and died afterward. I have worked in establishments that received bad reviews before— well, not for me, of course." He cocked his head in a proud manner. "Within a week, the crowd was usually back to normal.

The whole thing might have blown over in a few days, but his sudden death puts everything in a new light. I am certain that Detective Ray will be back to bother us again too."

"Keanu and his parents went down to the police station to talk to him. Ray questioned me this morning."

Poncho started to place the warm cookies in a plastic container. "Lucky you. Like we did not have enough trouble around here already with the register coming up short."

"How'd you know about that?" I asked.

"I overheard Keanu and Terry discussing it yesterday. They do not know that I heard them."

Sybil came into the kitchen and placed an order slip on the silver wheel located on the counter. Poncho glanced at it and immediately reached into the fridge for some chopped vegetables. He then poured some sesame oil into a steel frying pan, and added chopped chicken. I had no culinary skills to speak of, but it looked like he was preparing chicken teriyaki.

"What's your opinion on that?"

He stirred the pan's contents thoughtfully. "I do not like to single people out but would bet my life that it was not you or Vivian. So you do the math. Who is left?"

I already had my suspicions but, like Poncho, didn't want to spread any tales until I was certain.

My phone pinged with a text message. I glanced down and spotted Keanu's name. "I'll be back in a few minutes." I went into the small adjoining room for employees to read his text in private.

Stepped out of the room for a minute. Told Ray I needed a drink of water. Basically, he's grilling us about what exactly Dad said to Cremshaw on the phone this morning. Did my parents offer him free food, or maybe something else like money, so he'd forget about the blog post? My father is getting really pissed.

I started to type out a reply, but then another text from him arrived first.

I don't want to be here. I'd rather be lying on the beach somewhere, kissing my beautiful girlfriend.

His words made me smile. It had been such a crappy day for the both of us, but as always, the thought of Keanu was a bright spot, like the sun hidden behind clouds. I typed out: *I wish you were here. There's a cast party after the show tonight. Will you come with me, and then we can go back to my place?*

His response was immediate. *You know I will. I can't wait for us to have some alone time together and forget about the real world for a while.*

Me too. I could almost picture Terry trying to engage Ray in a shouting match and Keanu's useless efforts to calm his father down. Heck, I wouldn't have wanted to be there either.

It was bad enough that we were all considered suspects in Randolph's murder. On top of that, Keanu now had to deal with someone lifting money out of the register. I knew that Poncho suspected Coral, even though he hadn't said her name. Then I remembered Vivian's earlier comment about Coral being jealous of me. Had she really filled the ketchup holders with Tabasco sauce so I'd be blamed? Was she taking money in an attempt to get me into trouble? *No. Not everything's about you.* The entire thing sounded crazy, but still, what did I really know about the girl?

I glanced uneasily at the stairs that led to the office, and the naughty side of my brain had a sudden idea. On impulse, I climbed the stairs slowly and quietly so that Poncho wouldn't hear. The door was almost always left ajar, as Keanu liked the idea of an open-door policy for his employees. In such a short time as manager, he'd been wonderful at handling the staff. He knew how to listen and genuinely cared about his workers. Sure, I might be a bit biased, but it was difficult to find fault with the man.

There was a couch upstairs in the middle of the wooden paneled floor, with a couple of armchairs positioned by the oak desk in an attempt to form a seating group. A small coat closet was located in the corner of the room. Ava, who was always cold—even on 80-degree days like this—kept a sweater hanging in there. Two shelves above the coat rack held receipts, bank statements, and other accounting paraphernalia that I could never hope to figure out. Keanu also had an accounting degree, which served him well in the dual role of manager and financial expert.

I had no business being up here alone. One of my worst habits was my inquisitiveness, and it had almost proved fatal to me after Hale's death. I'd snooped around in Keanu's desk when it had previously been Hale's, curious about his murder and if one of my coworkers might have been responsible for it. I sat down in the swivel chair and reached for the bottom drawer, where I knew employee files were kept. It wasn't locked. I pulled the drawer open and searched for Coral's folder. I reminded myself that I wasn't going to look at anyone else's information, so this made it okay, right?

There was a day last week when I'd spotted Coral standing idly next to the register right before closing. I'd asked her if she'd wiped down the tables on the patio, and she'd muttered something about making change for a customer. I'd dismissed the episode afterward, but now started to wonder. What if Coral had been in the middle of removing money from the drawer when I'd interrupted her?

Coral's file stated that she lived in town, and her mother was listed as an emergency contact. Her résumé listed previous experience at an IHOP restaurant in Kauai, which had ended about a year ago, but nothing since, which I thought was a bit strange. Keanu surely must have called for references. I also noted that Coral was a student at Aloha Lagoon Community College.

If Coral was putting herself through school, it had to be difficult on a server's salary. I remembered Sybil saying something recently about her parents paying for her tuition and how grateful she was to them. Coral had overheard the conversation and muttered something under her breath about Sybil being a "pampered princess." I made a mental note to ask Sybil, who went to the same school, if she'd ever interacted with Coral on campus.

The temptation to tell Keanu about my suspicion was great, but I would need more proof first. He might have drawn the same conclusion as well if he'd looked at Coral's file. Plus, I didn't know how he'd react if I told him I'd been launching my own investigation. He was aware of my past snooping and most likely wouldn't want me involved.

I replaced the manila file in the drawer and closed it shut. As I rose from the desk, I heard footsteps and voices on the stairs.

"Dad, I don't have time for this right now," Keanu complained.

"Well, make the time. The restaurant is dead anyhow. Guess we'd better learn to expect that," Terry growled in return.

I froze in my tracks. Oh crap. *Crap!* They were headed upstairs to the office. How would I explain what I was doing here? My eyes darted around the room, and without thinking, I dashed into the closet and shut the door behind me. My heart thumped wildly against the wall of my chest, and then I cursed myself. *Why did I just do that?* I should have said I came upstairs to drop off a produce receipt or something like that. Now it was too late—I was trapped. I prayed they wouldn't stay long.

"Your *girlfriend* must be out on a break." Terry's voice was thick with sarcasm. "See, when the cat's away, the mouse will play."

I was stunned at his words. I'd always tried to be a good employee and had never given Terry a reason to think I was a slacker. Where was this coming from?

Keanu's tone was low, but I detected a note of anger in it. "She's not on the clock Dad, remember? She came to get her purse and decided to stay here until her show because she didn't want to be alone after what happened this morning. How can you be so insensitive?"

"She seems like a nice girl, Terry." Ava's soft voice filled the room. "We should have Carrie over for dinner soon. I'd like to get to know her better." She paused for a few seconds. "How serious are things between the two of you, dear?"

I held my breath and waited for his reply.

"Things are very serious," Keanu answered.

The entire room was silent except for the heavy breathing emanating from my body. In a sudden panic that they might hear my obscene phone caller–like noises, I clamped a hand over my mouth and struggled to breathe normal.

"She's a waitress, Keanu," Terry snarled. "A server. One of *our* servers, in fact. You would have been better off with the hula girl you dated before. Tammy, wasn't it?"

There was silence again, and I wondered if Keanu might be struggling for composure. He'd mentioned that they'd argued quite a bit recently but never told me about what. I'd assumed it had been over the restaurant, but now it didn't take a soothsayer for me to figure out that *I* was the main topic of their conversation.

"Son," Terry went on. "I know you feel like you're infatuated with this girl, but there are a lot of things that don't add up here. I saw her filling the ketchup containers the other day. Maybe she put Tabasco sauce in there for a joke. Plus, we have the recent thefts to consider. I really think—"

"Well don't," Keanu snapped, his voice sharp as a razor's edge.

I'd never heard him speak like that before and certainly not to his parents. I shrank back in the far corner of the closet, squatting down underneath the shelves as he continued.

"Carrie's no thief, and she would never fill the containers with Tabasco sauce as some type of sick prank. She's been through a lot in her life. She's the most caring and warmest person I've ever met—except for Kara."

My eyes started to water as I listened. Keanu had always spoken with such pride of the older sister whom he'd idolized and to be compared to her was the highest compliment. She'd been barely out of her teens when she'd moved to Oahu, an attempt to get out from under Terry's thumb and live with her boyfriend. A picture of the beautiful young woman graced one of the walls in the upstairs office, and her younger brother was almost an exact clone. Kara had long, flowing dark hair and those same incredible ocean blue eyes, with a smile that would steal anyone's heart.

The quiet was ominous and deafening. If I'd had more room, I would have squirmed with discomfort. This was an extremely personal family moment that I didn't want to be privy to.

Terry's voice was gruff. "Don't you dare compare her to your sister."

"It's the truth." Keanu said calmly. "Nothing's really changed since then, has it? You refuse to give Carrie a chance, just like you never gave Steve a chance. Kara loved him, Dad. It broke her heart that you didn't even try to get along with him. Why are you so set on doing this again?"

"Keanu don't," Ava implored. "Please."

"You're too young to know what you want," Terry replied. "Plus, you could do so much better. What if this girl is just using you? She knows you're going to inherit both businesses someday."

The words bit into me like a snake's venom and were just as painful. It took every bit of restraint on my part to keep from storming out of the closet and telling Terry straight to his face what he could do with both of his precious businesses.

"Don't do this, Dad," Keanu warned. "Don't drive me away. I'm twenty-six years old, and I know *exactly* what I want. At the top of the list is Carrie."

Ohmigod. His words warmed me from the top of my head to the tip of my toes.

"Keanu?" Poncho's voice came suddenly from below. "Is Carrie up there with you?"

I bit into my lower lip. *Damn it.* The good chef was about to blow my cover. *Nice going, Ponch.*

I heard someone walking across the wooden floor, and then Keanu spoke from a further distance away. "I haven't seen her. Why?"

"We were talking, and she went to take a phone call," Poncho explained. "I must have missed seeing her come back out. She forgot to take her cookies with her."

"She couldn't have gone far," Keanu said. "She has to leave for her show soon." There was the sound of footsteps again, and his voice became louder. "If we're done for now, I'd like to go find my girlfriend."

"Just a minute," Terry snarled. "What do you mean she's at the *top* of your list? What exactly are your intentions with this *server*?"

I shivered inwardly. The way Terry said the word made me feel dirty and vile, almost as if he was afraid I might give his son a disease.

Keanu must have shared my thoughts. "Don't talk about her like that, Dad. Her name is Carrie. Stop referring to her as our hired help, a server, or someone who's out to ruin the restaurant. She's my *girlfriend*. I'm crazy about her, and you need to get used to that."

"What does that mean? Are you in love with this girl?"

Terry wanted to know.

Keanu's answer came without hesitation. "Yes, I am."

My heart fluttered wildly at his words. Emotions of both joy and shock whipped through me like a strong ocean breeze and left me breathless. For a moment, I forgot where I was and staggered backward, my head connecting with the shelf. I let out an *oof* as pain thundered through my head.

The closet door was immediately jerked open. I was met by the unwelcome sight of Terry's angry eyes, which smoldered away like an inferno as they stared hotly into mine.

I was busted.

CHAPTER SEVEN

———

"Hello, Carrie," Terry greeted me sourly. "What a surprise. Is this the new break room? I hope we're not interrupting anything."

Keanu came into view behind his father and stood there, watching me with a puzzled expression. "Carrie, what are you doing in there?"

It was difficult to look into those gorgeous eyes and explain myself, especially with his father leering at me. Meekly, I emerged from my hideaway. "I'm sorry. I didn't mean to listen in. It was just that—um—"

"Maybe you were looking for some extra cash up here?" Terry placed his hands on his hips and continued to stare me down. "Perhaps you haven't made enough in tips lately to satisfy you?"

Keanu's face suffused with anger. "Dad, don't talk to her like that!"

Terry whirled around to face his son. "I think I have a right to know why this—*server*—was in my office eavesdropping on a private conversation."

"I didn't mean to listen in. That wasn't my intention." My face burned with humiliation as both men continued to stare at me, along with Ava. Finally, I couldn't stand it anymore. "I'm sorry." I ran across the floor and flew down the stairs.

"Carrie, wait!" Keanu yelled after me.

I'd had a good head start and no intention of stopping. This had to be one of the most humiliating moments of my life, and I just wanted to run as far away from it as possible. I was through the kitchen in a flash and almost knocked Poncho over in the process. I muttered a quick "Sorry!" and headed out the patio entrance, where I almost collided with a couple taking in a view of the ocean as they enjoyed their mai tais.

I continued running down the path that led to the ocean and vaguely recalled the last time I had done this—right after I'd found Hale's dead body. Back then I was sick to my stomach, terrified, and overwhelmed. Not much had changed since that incident three months ago, except for one constant thought that kept running through my head.

What will Keanu think of me now?

I was busy slipping my way through the sand when my arm was grabbed from behind. I whirled around and found myself staring directly into Keanu's puzzled face. He didn't look angry, but his expression was somber.

He spoke softly. "What was all that about?"

I didn't reply right away—first, because my chest was about to explode from the sprint I had just undertaken. I was not runner material and never had been. Second, I didn't have an answer for him.

Keanu waited for me to catch my breath. It occurred to me that he always seemed to be waiting for me in one way or another. Waiting to see how far I would take our relationship, waiting to pick me up or bring me somewhere, waiting for me to do something stupid, like what had just happened. His patience knew no boundaries where I was concerned, and to hear him profess his love for me had shaken me to the core, although it shouldn't have come as a surprise. Those eyes that bore into mine now—deep set with their vivid shade of blue rivaled only by the ocean—were my final undoing. I began to cry.

Keanu put his arms around me and stroked my hair soothingly. "Don't cry, Carrie. Everything's all right."

Embarrassed, I hiccupped back a sob. "How can it be? I'm a walking disaster. I wasn't trying to listen in on your conversation, honest."

He pulled back so that he could study my face and wiped my tears away with the pad of his thumb. "Will you at least tell me why you were hiding in the closet?"

Exhausted, I pressed my head against his rock-hard chest as his arms went around me protectively. I could have stayed like this forever. "I was snooping."

His body went rigid against mine. "Gee, that's a new one."

I took his sarcasm as a hopeful sign. "I think I have an idea who might be taking the money from the restaurant. Remember the time you knew I'd been looking at the employee files after Hale died?"

Keanu sighed heavily. "Carrie, not again."

I stared up into his face. "I know your father thinks it was me who filled the ketchup holders with Tabasco sauce. To be honest, I was also worried he might think I took the money."

He caressed my cheek with his fingers. "Don't worry. I'll set him straight."

"It won't matter because he won't listen. Your father doesn't like me. He—" I bit into my lower lip. "He thinks I'm beneath you."

Keanu placed his hands firmly on my shoulders. "I don't care what my father thinks. You are beneath *nobody*. Understand? No one is better than anyone else on this earth." He stared out at the ocean. "Dad means well, but he doesn't know how to relate to people anymore. He's kind of shut himself off from the world since Kara died."

His words made sense. Everyone had a different mechanism for handling grief, and I was determined not to pass judgment. Still, it seemed like Terry had no problem passing it my way though.

Keanu reached for my hand. "Come on." We started back up the path slowly, and then he cocked his head toward me. "You think Coral took the money, don't you?"

My jaw dropped. "How did you know?"

He ran a hand through his hair. "Because I've been thinking the same thing. Don't tell anyone, but we've installed a camera inside the restaurant. It's not one that can be easily spotted by the human eye. So we may have our answer in a day or two."

I squeezed his hand tightly. "Just make sure you put your hand over it so your parents don't catch us kissing again."

He roared with laughter and hugged me close. "How did I ever live without you?"

My sentiments exactly. I looked up and caught sight of

Sybil standing on the Loco Moco's patio. When she spotted us, she ran down the path in our direction.

"Carrie!" She was a pretty girl, with shoulder-length dark blonde hair and enormous green eyes set in a slim face. "Tad's out front waiting for you."

Cripes. I'd forgotten it was time to leave for the show. I pulled out my phone, and sure enough, there was a text message from Tad. *Your chauffeur awaits.* At this rate, we'd barely make it to the Hana Hou on time.

"Thanks, Sybil." I released Keanu's hand reluctantly. "But what about you? You've been here since early this morning. You must be exhausted."

Sybil shook her head. "Nah. It's been so slow all day I don't feel like I've done much. Plus, I can use the money…although some tips would make it even better, you know?"

She turned to go back inside the café, but I laid a hand on her arm. "Have you got a second?"

"Sure." She looked wide-eyed from me to Keanu. "What's up?"

I probably should have cleared this with Keanu first but felt certain he'd have my back. "You go to Aloha Lagoon Community College, right?"

She smiled proudly. "Yeah, I'm in my second year, and then I'm hoping to transfer to the University of Hawaii next fall. I'm majoring in psychology."

"That's great."

Keanu watched me, arms folded over his broad chest. It was obvious by the grin he flashed that he knew what I was up to. That gave me the courage to proceed. "Do you ever see Coral there?"

She made a face. "Yeah, I see her every once in a while but do my best to avoid her."

Keanu seemed intrigued. "Why is that?"

"She worked in the school's cafeteria for a while and then got fired. There's talk that she—" Sybil's face reddened, and she stared out toward the ocean. "I shouldn't be saying this."

I decided to help her out. "Were there rumors that she was stealing?"

Sybil hung her head. "I don't want to cause trouble for her at the café or make her mad, so please don't say it was me." She glanced at Keanu with alarm. "I like this job and want to keep it. At least until I know for sure if I'm able to transfer or not."

"There's nothing for you to worry about," Keanu assured her. "I won't tell my parents you said anything. Scout's honor."

Sybil turned back to me, her chin jutted forward. "Coral has a mean streak. Oh, and by the way, she hates you."

That was encouraging. "Why?"

She cut her eyes to Keanu and gave me a sly smile. "Three guesses."

If the entire situation hadn't been so serious, I might have laughed out loud. It all seemed so petty and juvenile. I'd only just turned twenty-five myself but already felt decades older than the other girls.

My phone beeped. "That must be Tad, getting impatient." I smiled gratefully at Sybil. "Maybe we can talk more later."

"Sure thing," she said and hurried back inside the café.

Keanu gave me a light kiss. "Knock 'em dead tonight, baby. I'll be thinking about you."

"Thanks for being so wonderful."

He grinned at me in a teasing manner. "It's just part of my job."

I laughed and hurried around the side of the building to where Tad was parked, drumming his fingers impatiently against the steering wheel of his white convertible.

"I was about ready to come in there and lift you over my shoulder like some evil caveman." Tad watched as I fastened my seat belt, and then he placed the car into drive. "You know Jeff hates it when anyone is late."

"You have permission to blame me. I'm really sorry, but there's a lot of stuff going on at the Loco Moco." I relayed to Tad what had happened with Randolph.

Tad clucked his tongue against the roof of his mouth. "Oh, I already heard, love. The entire island knows what's going on. So, tell me, who's the unlucky server who delivered the tainted food to the Kona man?"

I raised my hand and waved it in the warm wind.

"Shut up!" Tad slammed on the brakes and nearly missed hitting the back of a car that had stopped for a traffic light in front of us. "What is it with you and dead bodies, girlfriend?"

I shrugged. "Just lucky, I guess."

Tad raised an eyebrow at me as the light turned green. "I bet this doesn't bode well with the boyfriend's parents either. How bad was business today?"

"Let's say there wasn't any." My phone pinged, and I stared down to see I had a message from Vivian.

Call me as soon as possible!

My stomach lurched. Had Vivian gotten worse? Did she need me to take her to the hospital? What if someone had poisoned her too? What if—*Oh for crying out loud, Care. Your imagination is running away with you again.*

I pressed the Speed Dial button with Vivian's name, and she instantly picked up.

"Thank God."

"What's going on? Are you okay?"

Her voice was low. "I'm at the police station, on my way out."

Fear jolted through my entire body. "Why? What's going on?"

Her breath caught, and she sounded like she was trying to hold back a sob. "Oh my God, Care, you're going to hate me."

I couldn't stand it any longer. "Viv, please tell me what's going on."

"As soon as I left the Loco Moco, I got a phone call from Detective Ray, asking me to come down to the station." Vivian sighed heavily into the phone. "It seems that Terry and Ava gave Ray all the employee phone numbers when they were in earlier. So, you know what that means."

"He already questioned me," I said, a bit defensively.

"Yeah, well, he's going to be bothering you again, mark my words. And it's all thanks to me and my big mouth."

The day had already been a long one and was nowhere near being over with, so I struggled to keep the irritation out of my tone. "Will you please tell me what happened?"

"Detective Ray wanted to know what kind of contact I had with Randolph the other day when he came to the café," Vivian explained. "I mentioned how I'd brought the ketchup out to him and about the hot sauce incident. Then I told him how Randolph had asked for you this morning. I specifically made it known that you did not want to go to his room." Her voice quivered. "I thought I was helping, honest."

Tad looked over at me and rolled his eyes. "God, that girl can go on and on all day if you let her."

"I heard that," Vivian yelled.

I moved the phone away from my ear. "Okay. What happened when you told Ray that I went to Randolph's room?"

"Ray wanted to know the exact time," Vivian said. "So, I pulled my phone out and practically flung it at the good detective so he could check himself. The guy was really starting to bug me, you know?" She sniffed. "I forgot, Carrie. Honest to God, I forgot all about it, or I wouldn't have let him see the phone!"

"Forgot about what?" I was thoroughly confused now.

Vivian paused. "The text that you sent me. Remember when you left the room and asked me to have the coffee ready so you could bring it back to Randolph right away?"

"Of course I remember." Realization set in, and I gasped. "Hang on." I put Vivian on hold while I checked the text from earlier today. There it was, staring me in the face. I'd even put the message in caps to show how aggravated I'd been.

It's a wonder no one has killed this guy yet.

"Care?" Vivian's worried voice filtered through the phone. "Are you still there?"

My throat tightened. Oh man. Detective Ray couldn't possibly think it was me. Or did he? We'd been down this road before. If only—

"Carrie!" Vivian shouted.

Good grief. "It's okay, Viv." My phone pinged to let me know I had a new voicemail. "I appreciate you telling me this, but I'm sure everything will be fine."

Vivian sounded unconvinced. "I'm so sorry. I'd forgotten all about it until he pointed out the message. Swear to God."

"It's okay," I repeated. "Listen—Tad and I are at the theater now, and we're late. I'll call you after the show, all right?

Get some rest."

"Sure. Break a leg, hon." She disconnected.

"What gives?" Tad's catlike green eyes shone in the sun with curiosity.

I held up a hand while I checked my voicemail. Call me crazy, but I already had a premonition of who'd left me a message and it turned out that I was correct. When I heard the deep male voice on the other end, a rush of cold air blew through me, even in the hot Hawaiian sun.

"Carrie, this is Detective Ray Kahoalani. I realize you're in a production tonight, but I'd appreciate your stopping by the station afterward so we can have a little chat. I'll be here quite late—waiting for you."

CHAPTER EIGHT

————

"This guy is really starting to piss me off," Keanu muttered between clenched teeth as he gripped my hand tightly, and we walked toward the police station.

It was after eleven o'clock at night, but lights still shone from the single-story stucco structure in the middle of town where Detective Ray could be found lurking. For some odd reason, I found myself wondering what color Hawaiian shirt he would be wearing tonight.

I'd texted Keanu before the show and told him about Ray's voicemail. He'd insisted on coming along and was waiting for me outside when the show had ended. The entire cast was going out for drinks afterward, but I'd explained to Jeff that I needed to take a rain check since real life was calling.

Keanu didn't swear often but had muttered a few expletives on the phone as he wondered aloud why Detective Ray was determined to destroy me and his family's livelihood.

I only wanted this awful day to end. My arms still ached, although the ointment I'd been using had started to help. Plus, I couldn't remove the image of Randolph drawing his last breath from my head.

Exhaustion had seeped into my bones, and my performance tonight had been nothing short of terrible. On top of everything, Jeff had been in a real crappy mood as well. This was becoming the new norm in my life—everyone around me either seemed to be irritated or disliked me for some reason, such as Terry, Jeff, and Coral. The disgruntled mood had also transferred itself to Keanu, although I knew his anger wasn't directed at me.

Jeff had come backstage after the performance to tell me

and Jennifer—the woman who played Amy March, my character's little sister—that our performances were two of the most God-awful ones he'd ever witnessed during his entire career. To say that we'd both been stunned was an understatement. In fact, Jennifer had broken down in tears while Jeff was still there ranting, and then he'd merely walked away without another word. Needless to say, I wasn't exactly heartbroken that we would not be chatting together over drinks tonight.

I relayed the story to Keanu as we walked into the station, and he was furious. "I can't believe that jerk is giving you such a hard time. Did you tell Jeff that you found a dead body this morning? That's bound to affect anyone's performance."

"No. The first thing you learn as an actor is that there is no excuse for a bad performance. If you're suffering, the performance should be all the better." My high school director had quoted those famous words to me when I'd portrayed Laura in *The Glass Menagerie*, and they'd stuck with me ever since.

Keanu rubbed my arm. "Stop beating yourself up. Jeff needs to get over himself. It's not like he's directing a Broadway production."

I knew he was trying to make me feel better, but nevertheless, the words still hurt. Like any other show I'd ever been in, this one meant something. For me, acting was a passion. It must be similar to the way a writer felt about their book, or an artist about their painting. Keanu thought this was merely a hobby for me when in fact it was so much more. He didn't understand how consumed I was. No one did.

"It doesn't matter if it's Broadway or a rundown theater in a back alley somewhere," I replied. "An actor should never give less than his best performance."

Keanu blew out a sigh and pulled me against him. "I'm sorry, Care. I didn't mean it to come off like your show isn't important. You know how proud I am of you."

I kissed him on the cheek. "No worries. I understand." We were both worn out and frustrated with the events of the day. Neither one of us was jumping up and down at the thought of visiting the great detective either.

Keanu opened the door to the station. "Let's hurry up and get this over with. After we're done, let's go across the street to the coffee shop. When's the last time you ate?"

I didn't even remember. "Breakfast maybe?"

He looked startled. "No wonder your performance was off tonight. We've got to get some food into you."

"I just want to be with you. That's all that I need."

Detective Ray was at the front counter, talking in earnest to the man stationed behind it. They both glanced up as we entered the building, and Ray watched us approach with unbridled interest.

"Carrie, you made it." He nodded at Keanu. "I see that you decided to come back for more too."

Keanu's jaw stiffened. "I didn't want Carrie to come alone. She's had a long day."

"We all have," Ray said wearily as he motioned for us to follow him down the hall to his office. When we reached the doorway, I stared inside with equal parts of fascination and disgust. Detective Ray was a major slob. The desk was piled high with papers and a paper plate that held a half-eaten sandwich that had seen better days. Discarded paper coffee cups filled the overflowing trash can in the corner, and a file cabinet situated against the wall was buried underneath assorted books and papers. A philodendron in the opposite corner of the room looked like it hadn't been watered in weeks and was destined to die a slow death.

He nodded at the two padded chairs in front of his desk then stepped forward to clear a stack of papers off one of them. "Have a seat. Can I get either of you some coffee? Water?"

We both shook our heads.

"Okay, let's get down to business then." Ray leaned back in his chair. "First, there's the matter of that text you sent to Vivian."

"What text?" Keanu asked.

Detective Ray cleared his throat and read from a sheet of paper in front of him. "'*Tell Poncho that the jerk said the coffee's not hot enough. Have a new carafe ready to go when I get back. It's a wonder no one has killed this guy yet.*'"

Keanu sucked in a breath while I gripped the arms of my

chair. "*I* didn't kill him, Detective. What would have been my motive?"

Detective Ray tapped a pencil laced with teeth marks on the desk in front of him. "Maybe the blog comments he left about your boyfriend's café, which also happens to be your place of employment? Such a post could prove to be detrimental for their future business and your career."

"This is crazy," Keanu growled. "Carrie had nothing to do with Randolph's death, and neither did my parents. She already told you someone else had been in the room with Cremshaw."

"The mimosa glasses," I put in. "Were they checked for fingerprints?"

Detective Ray shook his head. "We found one glass, and only Mr. Cremshaw's fingerprints were on it."

"That means the person who killed Randolph took the glass when they left so they wouldn't incriminate themselves." I was thinking out loud again, another bad habit of mine.

Detective Ray deftly raised one eyebrow. "I guess I'd better watch my back. Looks like you're gunning for my job, Carrie."

Keanu frowned. "Are there cameras in the hallways at the resort?"

"Nope. Only by the elevators, and we already checked the footage." Detective Ray scratched his head. "Mr. Cremshaw's room was located directly next to the stairwell. Whoever did this chose the stairs as their exit route and managed to avoid the camera in the process."

I snapped my fingers. "What if they poisoned the mimosas? Have the drinks been tested yet?"

Detective Ray pressed his lips together tightly. "Miss Jorgenson, if you don't mind, I'll do the questioning. I'm the law, not you."

No need to be rude, Detective.

Ray sighed, almost as if he'd heard me. "The toxicology tests on Mr. Cremshaw haven't come back yet, but we're pretty certain we know how he died."

"Which was?" I prompted.

He stared at me thoughtfully. "It seems that the coffee

you served Mr. Cremshaw held something a bit more powerful than just cream and sugar. We found cyanide in it."

"So Dr. Yoshida's assumption was correct." An uneasy feeling swept over me. Whoever had been in that room with Randolph had slipped the poison into his coffee, I was certain. But how could I prove that it hadn't been me?

"Detective, I didn't do this. Was there cyanide found in the carafe as well?"

Detective Ray shook his head. "Only in the cup he'd been drinking out of. Miss Jorgenson, I'm afraid that I have to insist you don't leave town until we have further details regarding this case."

Keanu's face reddened. "Ray, how could you possibly think that Carrie is involved? She was the one who discovered Hale's killer a few months ago."

Detective Ray gave him a small sympathetic smile. "I'm sorry, but she had opportunity, and she had motive. What happened in the past doesn't count." He cut his eyes to me. "Don't worry. There isn't enough evidence to arrest you—yet."

What a cheerful thought. How could I prove to Ray that I was not involved with this fiasco? I racked my brain for something else to say and thought about the method of death again. "Detective, where could a person buy cyanide? I'm speaking figuratively, of course."

Ray shifted in his seat. "I don't know all the possibilities, but there's a chance it can even be bought online. At least it used to be possible. We're currently checking into some different theories."

I would have loved to know what he meant, but it was pointless to ask. Detective Ray was not about to take Keanu and me into his confidence, especially since he considered us suspects.

"Mr. Cremshaw must have made quite a few enemies," I said. "He didn't have a very likeable nature. All you have to do is look at his Twitter or Facebook accounts. He was always nitpicking about something or ready to start a fight."

My observation drew a smile from Ray. "You've been doing homework on Mr. Cremshaw, I see."

Eagerly, I leaned forward in my seat. "Does his wife

know about his death?"

Detective Ray gave me a disbelieving look and shut his notebook, as if suddenly afraid I'd see what was inside. "I'm sorry, Carrie, but I can't tell you anything."

Jeez, I'm only trying to help. "All right, what else do you need to know?"

Footsteps could be heard in the hallway, and someone cleared their throat behind us. I turned around. The young man who had previously been stationed behind the receptionist counter was standing in the doorway. "Sorry, Boss, but can I see you for a second?"

Detective Ray nodded and eased himself out of his seat. "Excuse me for a minute, kids. Be right back."

As soon as he left the room, I rose from my chair and walked around behind his desk. I wasted no time in flipping through his notepad.

"What do you think you're doing?" Keanu hissed.

I put a finger to my lips. "Keep an eye out for him."

"Carrie!" he whispered. "If Ray finds you snooping through his things, it's only going to make matters worse."

"Well then, you'd better make a great lookout, mister," I retorted.

Keanu stared at me for a moment, mouth open in amazement, then flashed his dimple. He shook his head and went to stand in the doorway. Keanu poked his head out around the corner and tried his best to act nonchalant by placing his hands inside his jeans pockets and whistling. *Ugh.* I had my work cut out trying to teach my boyfriend the basic art of snooping.

Too bad Ray hadn't become an artist. Some of his doodles really had potential. I stared down in fascination at the words *Carrie* and *cyanide* intertwined around what looked to be a coffee cup design. *How nice.* I flipped another page. "Ah. Here we go."

Keanu looked over in my direction. "What is it?"

I pulled out my phone and took a picture of the page. "B Davenport, Monday at 10:00 am. Room 707. Does that mean she's at Aloha Lagoon? Could they be meeting there instead?"

"I think that's doubtful, especially with all the reporters that have been hovering around the place like vultures since

Cremshaw's death." Keanu glanced out in the hallway again and then started toward me. "He's coming!"

Before I could even react, he pulled me around to the front of Ray's desk and started to kiss me passionately.

"Ahem," Detective Ray said in an irritated voice. "I hate to interrupt you lovebirds, but this is *my* office."

We broke apart, breathless, and Keanu grinned sheepishly at the man. "Sorry, Detective. We got carried away in the moment. You know what it's like."

Well played, Watson. There might be hope for him after all.

Detective Ray cocked a finely arched eyebrow at both of us then reached onto the desk for his notepad, which I had remembered to close, thank goodness. "That's all for tonight. It's late. Go home. But I'll be seeing you both soon."

"That was close," Keanu murmured as we left the building. "Good thing I can think fast on my feet, huh?"

"You were magnificent." I leaned my head wearily against his shoulder, and his strong arm went around my waist to support me as we walked across the street to the coffeehouse. "How do you feel about the dynamic duo teaming up to find another killer?"

His eyes sparkled in the semidarkness around us. "What did you have in mind?"

"Detective Ray is looking at your parents and me as possible suspects in Randolph's murder. Maybe you as well, so what other choice do we have? The sooner we know who did this, the sooner the restaurant can get back to normal." Not to mention our lives. "Vivian read that Randolph and his wife were having problems. What if we found Belinda and questioned her before Ray does tomorrow?"

He stroked his chin thoughtfully, where his normal five o'clock shadow had turned into a wild midnight stubble that I found quite sexy. "Don't you have a show tomorrow?"

"A matinee, but I don't have to be at the theater until noon. We could go to the Aloha Lagoon about nine o'clock and try to find out if she's staying there. Then we could track her down before she leaves to meet with Ray."

We took our seats in a bright red booth, and the server

handed us menus. I studied mine without really seeing it. "So are you game?"

Keanu glanced at me in amusement. "There's never a dull moment with you. Sure, I'm game. But there are several other hotels on the island that have floors which go up to seven, so she might be staying there as well. I know almost all of the Aloha Lagoon receptionists, so we'll ask around in the morning and see if someone's willing to help us out."

I took a healthy sip from my water glass. "Are you working tomorrow?"

He nodded. "I was supposed to be off but told Dad I'd come in for a few hours. Poncho will open, so I'll go over after we get done with our sleuthing. Seems like I work every day lately." He blew out a long, ragged breath and glanced up at me. "I'm not sure that I'm ready for all my parents have planned for me."

I reached across the table and covered his hand with mine. "Maybe you should talk to your father. Tell him how you feel."

Keanu made a face. "As you know, my father isn't a very good listener. But it's worth a shot. He'll be at the restaurant tomorrow afternoon, so maybe I'll try then." He snapped his fingers suddenly. "Hey, I know."

"What?" My appetite was back, and I couldn't decide if I wanted pancakes or a gooey grilled cheese sandwich.

His mouth turned upward into a teasing smile. "Maybe you should join me and Dad tomorrow."

I wrinkled my nose. "Right. Why would I do that?"

Keanu winked. "You could jump out of the closet and surprise him while we're busy discussing how he's going to run my life."

"For some reason, I think that's been done already," I remarked.

CHAPTER NINE

———

"What does Belinda look like? Do you have a picture of her handy?" Keanu asked as he held the front door of the lobby open for me.

It was shortly after nine o'clock on Sunday morning, but the Aloha Lagoon Resort's main lobby was already bustling with activity. I'd been inside the resort several times for various reasons in the past few months, but its immaculate condition and elegance never failed to impress me.

The entire hotel with its various shops and the restaurants—the Loco Moco and Starlight by the Lagoon respectively—was the size of a small town itself. There was a line of people who seemed mildly depressed standing in front of the reception area, and I surmised their time in paradise was up. Others were disheveled and weary looking, perhaps ready to begin their vacation after a long, tedious flight.

One of the best things about living in this beautiful state was that I didn't ever have to leave and wasn't even contemplating such a thing. I had no desire to return to Vermont and had already accepted the fact that I would probably never see my mother and sister again.

Area throw rugs in muted colors covered the polished tile floors while people relaxed on brightly colored fabric couches for taxis to the airport or buses to various excursions. The floor was so clean and spotless that it shone in the morning sunlight. Two bellmen were busy at another desk, organizing luggage to take to vacationers' rooms.

I studied the text that Vivian had sent me a little while ago and showed the picture to Keanu. "This is Randolph's wife, Belinda Davenport."

Keanu's eyes widened as he stared at the voluptuous looking blonde in a barely there bikini. I quickly moved the phone away, and he grinned. "She's beautiful, but I know someone who's got her beat."

My ego now appeased, I placed the phone back in the pocket of my shorts. "Okay, you're forgiven."

"She's a model, right? What would she want with him?"

"He was worth a lot of money," I said.

"It can't be as much as she made," Keanu protested. "Food critics make a decent living, but they're not rich. Plus, he wasn't exactly in Anthony Bourdain's caliber. There had to be something else."

"Well, Viv sent me some other information too." How I loved that girl. She was a celebrity groupie who was always fascinated by the lives that they led. Her apartment was chock full of copies of *People* and the *National Enquirer.* "Apparently Belinda hasn't had any modeling gigs in a couple of years. Not sure what that's about. Maybe her age? Randolph inherited a small fortune when his father died last year. His mother passed away right before his father, leaving Randolph as the sole benefactor. Viv said his brother and parents didn't get along. The will still hasn't gone through probate, and Randolph's brother is contesting it."

Keanu grimaced. "Sounds like Belinda could be a potential suspect, along with Randolph's brother."

"Isn't it a known fact that the police always look at the spouse first?" Well, besides me that is.

He grinned. "Ask Vivian if she has any information on the brother."

I tapped my phone and read the rest of the book-length text Vivian had sent me. "I'm way ahead of you. His brother's name is Richard, and he lives in Hawaii. They both grew up in Honolulu, but Richard has a house in Poipu."

Keanu's eyes sparkled with a mischievous expression. "Maybe we can talk to him too, Sherlock."

"It's all elementary, my dear," I teased.

He grabbed my hand and led me toward the reception desk. "Come on. I know the girl who's working today. She'll help us out."

A tall, skinny blonde was stationed behind the counter, talking to someone on the phone. She appeared younger than me and wore the hotel uniform of blue polo shirt with the Aloha Lagoon logo embroidered over her left breast pocket. Her name tag read *Summer*. The perfect name for a girl who lived in paradise.

She said "Goodbye. Enjoy your stay" to the party on the other end and glanced up. When her eyes focused on Keanu, I saw them brighten in delight. *Ugh.* I was starting to get used to seeing women act this way around him.

"Hi, Keanu," Summer said breezily. "Is everything okay in your room?"

Keanu's parents kept a suite year round in the resort. When I had briefly needed a place to stay a couple of months back, he'd been kind enough to offer the room to me. He'd always come through for me in a big way and never let me down. The word *unreliable* was not in his vocabulary.

"Just fine," he said and gestured at me. "Summer, this is Carrie. We were wondering if you might help us out with something."

"Of course." She smiled at me. "What do you need?"

Keanu leaned forward on the marble counter. "Can you tell us if Belinda Davenport has left the hotel yet this morning?"

I loved Keanu's tactics. He didn't ask if Belinda was staying there, just made it appear that we already knew her whereabouts.

Her pleasant face twisted into a frown. "Sorry, but I'm not supposed to reveal any information about her while she's staying here. She's requested total anonymity."

Thank you, Summer. That was all we needed to know.

Keanu gave her a long, sexy smile. "Of course. I understand. We know she's in suite 707 but didn't want to head up if we'd already missed her. She's got a full morning ahead of her."

Her mouth opened in surprise. "Oh, I'm sorry. I didn't realize you were friends with her."

"I don't know her that well," Keanu admitted, "but she has a relationship with my parents, and we need to discuss a few things."

That was putting it mildly.

Summer shrugged her skinny shoulders. "She requested room service from Starlight this morning. I know the server who brought her tray up. He stopped to talk to me on his way back to the restaurant and mentioned that she didn't even bother to tip him. I haven't seen Miss Davenport in the lobby yet, but she could have left while I was busy with guests. Do you want me to ring her room for you?"

Keanu straightened up. "Not necessary, thanks. I'll let Mom and Dad know."

He gave her another winning smile while Summer flushed appreciatively and lowered her eyelashes. The man did know how to pour on the charm when necessary. It had to be a gift. "Have a great day," he said.

"You too." Her phone rang, and I heard her light, airy voice speaking into it while we walked toward the elevator. "Good morning. Aloha Lagoon Resort. How may I assist you?"

"At least we know she's here," Keanu said as we got into the elevator. "And I have another idea."

"You're just full of them this morning," I teased.

When we reached the seventh floor, Keanu let me go ahead of him, but as I started in the direction of Belinda's room, he suddenly caught my arm. "What are we going to say to her?"

"I have a plan, don't worry." It was quite a ridiculous one but all I had to work with right now. Hopefully, we could pull it off.

As we started down the hallway, a tall, willowy blonde stood in the doorway of suite 707, talking to someone in a raised voice. Curiosity nagged at me. Who was in Belinda's room? Another man? That wouldn't exactly be discreet behavior for a woman whose husband had just been killed.

"Let's wait by the elevator," Keanu suggested and led me back in the direction of the rattan chairs.

A few seconds later, Belinda passed us in an obvious huff. She wore a pair of silver stiletto sandals that were at least four inches high and an expensive black halter dress studded with rhinestones. Her long blonde hair was swept up in a French twist. The woman reeked of elegance, and her figure was excellent. Her face, however, was drawn so tight underneath the carefully applied makeup that I wondered if she'd had one too many Botox treatments.

As Belinda rang for the elevator, she glanced suspiciously at me. Then her eyes traveled to Keanu and did a full body scan.

Here goes nothing. I cleared my throat. "Miss Davenport, how excellent. I was just coming to look for you."

She gave me an icy blue stare. "Who the hell are you? Another reporter? Get lost, and let me grieve in peace."

Call me crazy, but the woman didn't appear to be grieving as she removed a compact from her purse and applied a careful coat of lip gloss to her overly plump lips.

I plodded on. "My name is…Chelsea. I work for Ron Howard." *Where the heck did that come from?* I had been tempted to give Howie's name, but there was a chance she knew him through her husband.

Belinda's eyes almost bugged out of her head. The elevator dinged, and the door opened, inviting her to enter, but she chose to ignore it. "Ron Howard? You mean, the director? A.k.a. Richie Cunningham?"

"The one and only," I assured her.

She studied me carefully. "He's here? In Hawaii?"

"Oh yes. Mr. Howard adores a tropical climate."

Her eyes moved to Keanu again, and I thought I spotted some drool collecting in the corner of her mouth. "And who might this gorgeous hunk be?"

"Victor," I said hurriedly, afraid that Keanu might screw something up. He wasn't as good at the lying gig as me. "He's Ron's key grip boy."

Keanu stared at me, puzzled, then smiled and gave Belinda a perfunctory bow. "Nice to meet you, Miss Davenport. If you get the part, it would be an honor to carry your bags anywhere."

Head smack. I elbowed him in the side and gave a small laugh to cover up the awkwardness. "Such a kidder. He meant that he looks forward to shooting you at the perfect angle with the cameras. Isn't that right, Vic?"

Keanu got the message and nodded, careful not to say anything further.

Belinda glanced from Keanu to me. "What picture is this?"

Oh boy. Now I'd really painted myself into a corner. Keanu stared at me with a sly smile that seemed to say, *Let's see you get out of this one.* I had never been creative at making things up on the spot, and the first image that popped into my mind was of Benny. "Uh, it's called *Nine Lives.*"

To my surprise, Belinda looked intrigued. "Really? A comedy?"

I shook my head. "No, a thriller. Ron's producing it himself. Anyhow, he thinks you'd be perfect for the part of waitress Vivian. Do you have a card I can give him?"

She reached into her black leather Gucci bag and handed me a business card that I surveyed with interest. *Belinda Davenport, model and actress for hire.*

"When should I expect his call?" she asked eagerly.

"Oh, anytime now," I said. "Maybe even within the next hour."

Belinda made a face. "Shoot. I'm headed over to the police station to meet with some stupid detective about my husband's death. I won't be available until this afternoon."

Here was the opportunity we were looking for.

"We were very sorry to hear about that," Keanu put in.

The pencil-thin eyebrows rose slightly as her eyes traveled down Keanu's physique and then slowly—very slowly—back up until she met his gaze and rewarded him with an adoring smile. "My goodness, Victor. How old are you, doll?"

The color rose in Keanu's cheeks. "Twenty-six, ma'am."

She licked her lips. "That's only a 15-year difference. No big deal."

I clenched my teeth together in irritation. "Um, Mr. Howard sends his condolences about your husband."

Belinda waved a hand impatiently. "Tell him thanks, but it is what it is." She studied her French-manicured nails as if the topic now bored her. "To tell you the truth, I'm not surprised. No one liked him very much. Some days I had trouble myself."

Wow. Tell us how you really feel. "Do you have any idea who might have killed him?"

She frowned. "Well, that locomotive restaurant is at the

top of my list. Apparently Randy said some nasty things about the place, so the owners obviously wanted him dead. Once all the tests come back on him, my lawyer will be slapping a big-time lawsuit on that piece-of-crap establishment."

A muscle ticked in Keanu's jaw, and I found myself holding my breath. It must have been difficult for him to listen to Belinda insulting the Loco Moco, but he said nothing.

"Anyone else?" I prompted.

"There's too many to count, honey. He's got enemies going back to his college days, maybe even before. Anyhow, what is this, the Spanish inquisition?"

Footsteps sounded behind me, and I turned around. A tall, slim man with light brown hair pulled in a ponytail was approaching us. He had dark eyes set in a serious face with a pale skin tone. He looked to be around Belinda's age. There was something distinctly familiar about him, especially his eyes, but I couldn't quite place it.

He ignored both of us and placed a hand on Belinda's shoulder. "I'm sorry, but I had to take that call. I didn't think you'd still be here."

Anger flashed in Belinda's crystal clear blue eyes. "Go back to your lousy phone. I don't need you." She rang for the elevator and then noticed Keanu and me watching in obvious interest. Her face colored slightly. "Uh—this is my brother."

The man's dark eyes widened in surprise, but he gave us both a curt nod. Belinda addressed him again. "You can't come anyway. It would look...bad."

The elevator pinged, and Belinda hurried inside. "Tell Ronnie I'll be waiting for his call." Her eyes lingered on Keanu one last time before the door closed.

Keanu turned toward Belinda's so-called brother and stretched out his hand. "Hi, I'm Victor."

The man merely grunted and turned on his heel, walking back in the direction of Belinda's suite.

"What the hell was that about?" Keanu wanted to know.

I twisted my long braid around my fingers, a perpetual habit of mine when I was nervous. "No idea. For some strange reason, I don't think that was Belinda's brother though."

Keanu folded his arms across his chest, and his face

grew pensive. "Boyfriend, perhaps?"

I nodded, the familiarity of the man nipping away at my brain like a woodpecker. "I feel like I've seen him somewhere before."

Keanu's phone pinged, and he drew it out of his pocket. His expression grew stern as he read the message silently and typed out a quick response.

"What's wrong?" My first thought was that someone else had died. Unfortunately, that was the way my life rolled lately.

He sighed in frustration and rang for the elevator. "That was Dad."

My biggest fan. "What'd he say?"

"He and my mother are flying to Arizona today. There's a problem with one of the supermarkets. If all goes well, they'll be back by tomorrow. I've got to get over to the restaurant right away."

Too bad I wasn't working today. The place was always so peaceful when Terry wasn't around. "What sort of problem?"

"It seems that the manager in Phoenix has forgotten how to manage," Keanu quipped. "Two of the employees had a fist fight last night. It was over something ridiculous, but the morale there is almost nonexistent. Mom and Dad want to meet with all of the employees in the entire store and at the other location nearby." He ran a hand through his hair as his phone pinged again, and then swore softly under his breath.

"Now what?" At least the messages didn't concern me.

Keanu typed out a reply. "My father checked the footage from the camera this morning, and it caught one of our employees with some very sticky fingers. He wants me to talk to this *person* while they're gone. Great fun that's going to be."

Uh-oh. "Is this who I think it is?"

He grimaced. "Yeah. It seems the camera caught our friendly server Coral with her hand in the till, removing a pile of fifties and twenties."

CHAPTER TEN

―――――

"He was in the audience this afternoon, you know," Rose remarked.

"Who are you talking about?" I hung my costume on a wire hanger in the wooden closet then tossed the pinafore apron and bonnet onto the shelf above it. It was a relief to be out of that dress. It itched to no end, and the fabric was heavy and uncomfortable. No wonder women from the 1800s always looked miserable in those black and white photographs.

Rose was sitting at the makeup table that we shared with the other girls. She brushed her sun-streaked blonde hair over her shoulders and smiled with satisfaction. "Howie Livingston, of course. Seriously, was there anyone *else* in the audience that mattered? I was spot on with my performance today too. He even stopped me afterwards to tell me what a great job I had done."

"Congratulations, that's terrific." I pulled on my T-shirt and jeans. Right now, my mind was preoccupied with other things than the show, such as the fact that Detective Ray was taking a good hard look at me and the Loco Moco.

Rose continued to watch me in the mirror, a smug look on her face. "Did he say anything to you?"

"No." Rose was okay—a little stuck on herself perhaps, but hey, if Howie wanted to transport her off to Hollywood, I wished her well. I always tried to look at life with the *glass is half-full analogy*. Maybe if Rose left, I'd get a lead role in the next production.

There were no more performances until Friday, five days away. Jeff had mentioned that he might call us in for a rehearsal one night, but other than that, we were on our own until the weekend. Thank goodness for small favors. As much as I loved performing, everything had begun to wear on me, and I needed a breather. Plus, I was scheduled to work every day this coming week. The rehearsals and performance schedule had been cutting into my pay, and I sorely needed the money.

Keanu was picking me up at my apartment in about an hour, and we were going out to dinner tonight. Afterward he'd planned to head over to Coral's house to speak with her. She'd called in sick today, and because of my absence, Keanu had been forced to ask Anna to come in again. Keanu had told me in an earlier text that he'd had enough of Coral's antics. This was the first time he'd ever had to fire an employee, and I knew he wasn't looking forward to it. Still, he readily accepted the fact that it was his job, and these things came with the territory. Keanu would be fine. In my opinion, there didn't seem to be anything he couldn't handle.

My heart swelled with pride as I thought about my boyfriend, and every day I fell a little harder for him. Although I wouldn't admit it to anyone, I was scared of my feelings and uneasy about giving my heart away. It had been broken so many times during the course of my life that I wasn't sure it could be repaired again.

"Did you hear what I said?" Rose asked, her voice tinged with impatience.

I jerked myself out of my thoughts. "Oh sorry, no."

"I overheard Howie tell Jeff that he wanted to get together tomorrow and discuss some *things*." Her face glowed. "Maybe I'll get a call to come and meet with them."

"Good luck. I hope it works out."

"Yoo-hoo!" Tad's voice resonated from the other side of the dressing room door. "Is everyone decent in there?"

I grinned. Tad was the breath of fresh air I sorely needed right now. "Come on in."

Tad opened the door. He was still wearing his Hana Hou T-shirt and a pair of faded blue jeans. He gave Rose a prissy smile that she returned and then addressed me. "Ready to go, love?"

"I think so." I turned around to say goodbye to Rose, but she was already on her cell, chatting to someone about how terrific her performance had been.

"Phew," Tad complained as we descended the stairs to the lower level. "That chick is so self-absorbed it makes me want to gag. You should have seen her fawning all over Howie after the show. Positively sickening."

"Well, it sounds like he might be interested in her. I understand how excited she must be." Seriously, it had to be a dream come true and difficult for me to not be envious of her.

"I thought you were terrific today, hon," Tad said. "You were off yesterday, which is understandable after what happened. But today you totally rocked the house."

I squeezed his arm. "Thanks. I needed to hear that."

We passed in front of Jeff's office, as his angry voice sounded from the other side of the door. "Seriously, what do you want from me?"

We exchanged glances with each another. No one else was around, and my curiosity swelled to the size of Rose's ego. Jeff might not be the easiest person to get along with, but he was also the best director I'd ever had. Sure, he'd yelled at me yesterday, but that was part of the job

"I know he came to see you," another man answered. There was something familiar about his voice, but I couldn't place it.

Tad pointed his finger at the closed door and whispered. "Howie?"

I shook my head. The voice didn't belong to Howie.

"Yeah, Howie and I had lunch with him on Friday," Jeff said. "The day before—" He paused. "What's your point?"

"I just want to make sure that I get what's coming to me." The anonymous male voice spoke stiffly.

Jeff's voice now resembled a low, angry growl. "Your axe to grind has nothing to do with me. Randy and I haven't been close in years."

"Maybe not," Mr. Anonymous said, "but if he has a stake in this theater, like Howie does, I'm entitled to his share."

There was silence for about thirty seconds. When Jeff spoke again, his menacing tone sent ice crystals through my veins. "This is a small community theater. What the hell do you think, that I make millions here? Yeah, he wanted to be an investor, and I told him no. For your information, Howie doesn't have a share either. He's still thinking about it. So I don't owe *you* anything. You have no papers or anything else to prove ownership because they don't exist. Anyhow, why would you even care about my hole-in-the-wall theater? You've got bigger fish to fry."

"What's that supposed to mean?" the man asked.

Jeff chuckled. "I've heard the rumors about you and Belinda. I'm sure the press has too. If I were you, I might disappear from the island for a while. It's only a matter of time before the police get wind of your relationship, if you get my drift."

Tad's eyes nearly bugged out of his head. He had that look on his face that plainly said, "I know a secret!" Tad was the proverbial town gossip, and as much as I adored him, the fact remained that he couldn't keep anything to himself, even if his life depended on it.

"Are you threatening me?" Mr. Anonymous demanded.

"No," Jeff replied. "Frankly, I don't care what you and Belinda do. I don't want anything to do with this mess. Now if you don't mind, I have more important things to attend to."

Before Tad and I could move, the door was jerked open. *Cripes.* Both men stared out at us in surprise. This was the second time in as many days that I'd been caught snooping. I might get a reputation if this kept up.

The man began to move past us, but his eyes rested on mine for a moment, and I wondered if he'd recognized me. Now I knew why the voice had sounded familiar. It was the man who'd been talking to Belinda by the elevator this morning. *Who is he?*

Jeff narrowed his eyes. "Was there something you two wanted?"

Homina, homina, homina. Okay, how to get out of this one. *No, we don't want anything, Jeff. We were only listening in on your conversation.*

Tad swallowed hard. "Uh, Jeff, *I* wanted to see you. I was wondering if you might be available for drinks later."

God bless Tad. Jeff wasn't married, and I had no idea of his relationship status. He was a good-looking guy, but I honestly didn't know if Tad was his type or not. I'd thought that

Tad might prefer Gary, but who really knew? Anyone was fair game as far as Tad was concerned.

Jeff's stern face broke out into a wide smile. "Ah. Thanks, Tad, but my girlfriend is expecting me."

"Damn," Tad cursed under his breath. "Well, it was worth a shot."

I had to know. "Who was that man? I saw him at the Aloha Lagoon Resort this morning."

The smile on Jeff's face faded. "What was he doing there?"

I probably shouldn't have mentioned the encounter, but it was too late now. "I saw him with Randolph Cremshaw's wife."

Jeff frowned. "Obviously, you heard about his death. The man you just saw is his brother."

I should have guessed. "Richard Cremshaw?"

"How'd you know his name?" Jeff asked, surprised.

"I was the one to find Randolph after he died. The police questioned me, and then I learned he had a brother who lived in Hawaii. Please don't tell anyone about my finding Randolph," I added quickly. "The Loco Moco has already been affected enough by his blog."

Jeff scratched his head thoughtfully. "Wow. I heard that he'd died after a food delivery—it's all over the island. But I never made the connection with the Loco Moco, or that *you* were the one who delivered it. I thought it might have been Starlight."

I shook my head. "No such luck."

"That had to be a horrible experience for you, Carrie." Jeff suddenly looked sheepish. "I shouldn't have yelled at you last night. Why didn't you tell me what had happened?"

My face grew warm. "I didn't want to make excuses for my performance. You were right—I *was* off."

"Well, you certainly had your reasons," Jeff muttered.

I felt comfortable enough now to ask the other question that had been racing through my head. "How did you know Randolph?"

Jeff folded his arms across his chest. "We went to college together—Howie, Randolph, and me. Richard went there as well. He was two years behind us."

"Is he really involved with Randolph's wife?" I asked.

He narrowed his eyes. "You *were* listening in on our conversation."

Oops. I plodded on, trying to ignore his accusation. "I'm pretty sure they were in the same hotel room together. He came out right after she did. Do you think they could have been involved in his death?"

Jeff pressed his lips together in a stubborn manner. "Carrie, I don't want to comment on this. To be honest, I don't know much. Howie and I had lunch with Randy the day before he died. Randy was interested in becoming an investor in my theater. Then again, he might have only been interested because he knew Howie was thinking about it as well. He was like Howie's shadow, always following him around."

"Was he looking for a part in Howie's next picture?" I couldn't imagine why else Randolph would be so interested in the man.

Jeff shook his head. "I think Randy hoped Howie might help him get his own talk show started."

"Did Howie dislike him too?" Tad asked eagerly.

Jeff glared at him. "Howie doesn't dislike anyone. He's one of the nicest guys I've ever met. You'd be hard pressed to find anyone who actually liked Randy, especially anyone who owns a restaurant. He's reviewed almost everyone in this state."

"Not the Loco Moco," I remarked.

"Don't get me wrong," Jeff said. "The Loco Moco has fantastic food, but it's not exactly fine dining. Something more of Randy's caliber would have been Starlight by the Lagoon. It's a known fact that the manager there can't stand him. Randy told me that the guy punched him out last year after his latest review of the place hit *Dining Is Divine*."

Tad's eyes were round as saucers. "*Dining Is Divine*? That's like—the most popular cuisine magazine around. Bobby Flay was featured in it last month!"

My ears perked up while I processed Jeff's latest tidbit of information. Keanu knew the manager of Starlight, Jonathan Skyler. Then again, Keanu pretty much knew everybody who was associated with the resort in any shape or form because of his position at the Loco Moco and his parents. Every time we dined there, we received a premier table. Maybe we could go there for dinner tonight and have a little chat with Jonathan."

Jeff glanced at his watch. "If you two are done interrogating me now, I'm off to meet my girlfriend."

"Sorry to have kept you," I said.

Jeff moved back into his office. "Carrie, I'm taking the actors out on Friday night for drinks after the show, so please try to be available this time."

Cripes. This guy was like a faucet, on and then off again before I could blink an eye. *Why the attitude?* "That sounds great, Jeff."

He gave us both a thumbs-up. "See you guys later."

"Well," Tad huffed as we made our way to his car. "How nice that he didn't even bother to invite me to the soiree."

Good grief. "I'm sure he wouldn't mind if you came along."

"Hmm." Tad pouted openly as he arranged the Dolce and Gabbana sunglasses on his face. "I don't go where I'm not wanted."

"Stop being so sensitive." Heck, I would have been willing to let Tad go in my place. I'd spent more than enough time with Jeff lately.

Tad stuck his nose proudly in the air and pulled his car out of the parking lot and onto the main road. "Where are we headed, love?"

"You can drop me off at my apartment. I need to change before I meet Keanu for dinner."

His green eyes sparkled like jewels. "How is that gorgeous boy toy of yours?"

Tad always knew how to put me in a better mood. "He's fine. *We're* fine, actually."

"You two make such a cute couple," he cooed. "But be careful. I've seen the way Coral looks at him. She even posted something cryptic on Facebook the other day saying that the only good thing about her job was the hot-looking manager."

My head turned. "You're friends with Coral on Facebook?"

He tossed his head. "Of course. I'm friends with *everyone*."

I didn't doubt it. Tad was a Facebook junkie and posted

about everything from the weather to what not to wear when out clubbing. He had about 4,000 friends compared to my measly one hundred. I'd noticed that he even had friends who posted on his timeline asking for advice on romance or fashion. He was the Ann Landers of our generation.

I was dying to get a look at Coral's Facebook page. "Can I see your account for a second?"

He grabbed his phone from the console and handed it to me, eyes still fixed on the road. "My *face* is an open *book* for you, love."

I suppressed a laugh and started scrolling through his list of contacts. After a minute, I grew impatient and finally just typed the letter *C* in and found Coral after making my way through about one hundred Cathys, Carlas, and Cindys.

"So what about you and that gorgeous hunk of man you're dating? Hey, doesn't the K-man belong to a baseball team?"

I wondered where he was going with this. "Yes, but he hasn't played in a while. Too much work at the restaurant."

Tad grinned impishly. "But has he hit a home run with Miss Carrie Jorgenson yet?"

"Good God," I muttered. "Not you too. Come on. Some things are private, you know?"

"Look, honey. We all want the juicy details," he said. "Do you think you guys will get married?"

This startled me. "No idea. Nothing like jumping the gun, right? We've only been dating for a few months, Tad."

"Ah." He waved a hand dismissively. "Some people get married after only a few weeks. Yours is a case of true love at first sight."

"You're a born romantic," I teased.

He nodded. "I am, love. Truly, I am. It's plain to see the man is crazy about you. How do you feel about him?"

I hesitated for a moment. Tad's legendary blabber mouth was getting in the way of my admission. "I…I care for him very much."

"Oh," he mocked. "You *care* for him very much. This isn't *Little Women*, sweetheart, so lose the pathetic dialogue. Just admit you want to sleep with the guy."

"Tad!"

I found Coral's profile and clicked on it. The very first post that caught my eye almost made me drop the phone. "Check this out. 'I work with the biggest bunch of losers on the island.'"

Tad giggled. "Guess she didn't get the memo about not dissing your job on social media."

Maybe it didn't matter because I doubted that she would be employed at the Loco Moco for much longer. I clicked on her picture albums and started scrolling through the photos.

"You should get your cutest little nightie," Tad went on, "and then show up on K's doorstep at midnight. Wear yellow. It looks good with your skin tone."

"I hope you're kidding."

"Oh fine, pink will do."

Frustrated, I shook my head. "Can you please get your mind out of the gutter for a second? I'm not going to…"

I stopped in midsentence and stared down at the current picture on Tad's phone. It was of a little girl who bore a distinct resemblance to Coral. She was standing next to a tall man wearing a straw hat and glasses. Both looked extremely uncomfortable in the photograph.

My mouth went dry. "Ohmigod. Look what I just found."

Tad pulled over to the curb and took the phone from my outstretched hands. His eyes widened, and he whistled low in his throat. "Holy pineapples. Is that who I think it is?"

I nodded. "Yes. The one and only Randolph Cremshaw."

CHAPTER ELEVEN

———

Keanu glanced at his watch. "Jonathan is usually here around dinnertime. I wonder why we haven't seen him yet."

We were seated inside the charming Starlight by the Lagoon. The view of the ocean was spectacular from our table, strategically placed so that we were also able to see anyone who entered the restaurant. Being a people watcher, I enjoyed the combination. The place was packed as usual, and I'd overheard the hostess tell someone that there was at least a half hour wait for a table. Reservations were highly recommended.

Starlight wasn't a place that I could readily afford on my server salary. The only times I'd been here before was with Keanu. He always insisted on paying, and that sometimes bothered me. Yes, he was rich, and I was his girlfriend, but tonight my mind kept replaying Terry's outburst from yesterday. The words "gold digger" had been branded into my brain.

Keanu looked up from the ahi tuna he was eating and frowned. "What's wrong, sweetheart?"

"Nothing, I'm fine."

He pointed at my plate. "You've barely touched your food. Is something wrong with it?"

"No, everything is terrific as usual." I loved the mahi-mahi that was prepared with basmati rice and grilled vegetables. The restaurant was in a class by itself. Sure, the Loco Moco had delicious food, and Poncho was one of the best chefs on the island, but Starlight was your elegant, *take a girl here to wine and dine her* kind of place, while the Loco Moco was more of the *did you want extra barbecue sauce with your pulled pork* kind of establishment. The Loco Moco also came with extra perks, such as Poncho hollering from the kitchen or Vivian ogling every guy who walked through the door.

Starlight's motif resembled the ocean in its muted coral and turquoise colors. The elegance of the sophisticated restaurant was in its simplicity, which included the mild-mannered waitstaff and the tinkle of real silver that paired nicely with the soft piano music playing in the background. No matter how many times I'd been here, I'd never ceased to marvel at its chicness. Brad made a good living as a surfing instructor but had never taken me to a place like this while we'd been dating. His preferences ran more to the likes of Pizza Hut and McDonald's.

Keanu was still watching me with those gorgeous eyes that I considered my own personal ocean. "You're so good to me."

His face creased into a broad smile. "Nothing's too good for my lady. I hope you're still not thinking about my father and what he said yesterday."

How did he always know these things? "Well…"

He brought my hand to his mouth and kissed it while my insides quivered. "I love my father, but he doesn't always know best. I'm sorry you had to hear that. If it makes you feel any better, he's never really liked anyone I've dated."

How encouraging. Somehow, I couldn't picture the four of us having an amicable dinner together. It was made even more awkward by the fact that I was their employee. I decided to change the subject—slightly. "How did they come to live in Hawaii?"

Keanu drained his water glass. "I told you my great-grandmother was Hawaiian, right? My mother came here from Nevada to go to college and lived with her while she was in school. She then got a job in Arizona immediately after graduation, and that's where she met my father. Even though they settled there, she always wanted to come back to the islands. When Kara was about ten, my great-grandmother died and left Mom her house. She was pregnant with me at the time, so after I made my grand entrance into the world, they took off for tropical paradise and never looked back."

Before I could reply, I caught sight of Jonathan making his way toward us. He was about five ten, with dark brown hair and gray eyes set in a narrow face. As always, he was impeccably dressed in a lightweight khaki suit. His white teeth gleamed as he smiled at us.

Keanu had once mentioned that Jonathan had a financial share in the restaurant, although I knew the resort and Starlight were both owned by Freemont Hospitality. The Loco Moco was one of the few businesses in the Aloha Lagoon Resort that was owned independently.

"Keanu." Jonathan spoke in a suave voice and extended his hand in greeting. "How good to see you and your lovely girlfriend." He smiled politely. "I heard you were asking about me."

Keanu gestured at the empty chair between us. "Can you join us? I'd like to pick your brain for a minute."

Jonathan looked surprised but immediately sat down. "Of course. Let me guess." He winked at me. "You guys are planning a wedding and want to use Starlight for the reception."

My face must have turned about ten different shades of red.

Keanu, to his credit, only smiled and shook his head. "We're not quite there *yet*. But you never know." He raised an eyebrow at me, and my heart melted faster than an ice cream cone on the beach. "We wanted to ask you about Randolph Cremshaw."

The smile on Jonathan's face turned upside down. "What about him?"

"You must have heard about the incident in his room yesterday."

Jonathan nodded gravely. "I'm guessing business at the Loco Moco must be almost nonexistent because of...*him*. But don't worry. Mr. Cremshaw left us a crummy review—twice. After about a week, business started to pick back up again."

I tried to keep my expression neutral but couldn't believe the lack of remorse he showed over Randolph's death. Jeff had mentioned that Jonathan disliked the man. The question was, how much?

Keanu placed his napkin by the side of his plate. "Did you know him personally or just from his reviews?"

Jonathan cocked his head to one side and studied him closer. "Why are you asking me about that joker, Keanu? Are you suggesting I had it in for him?"

"I'm not suggesting anything," Keanu replied. "My parents may be looking at a possible lawsuit."

Jonathan's face was stern. "Oh wow. His wife is behind it, isn't she? Or shall we say his so-called wife? I've seen the tabloids. Would you believe that Miss Davenport had the nerve to come in a few nights ago, right before we were closing? We served her, but it was quite an inconvenience. Then she had a few drinks and refused to leave. Finally, some guy came in, talked to her for a few minutes, and escorted her out."

Keanu frowned. "What night was this?"

Jonathan paused to think. "Either Wednesday or Thursday night. I could check the receipts if necessary. I do happen to remember that her credit card was declined, and the guy she was with ended up paying for her meal."

I leaned forward. "What did he look like? Did you happen to catch his name on the receipt?" I wondered if it had been Richard.

He shook his head. "No, he paid cash. A rarity these days, but it does happen occasionally. The man didn't come in with her—he arrived after she'd finished eating and then sat down at her table. Let's see. He had reddish hair, glasses, and was kind of plain looking. Not the type of guy I'd expect to see her with. Then again, she was married to Cremshaw, so there's no accounting for her taste."

A chill ran down my spine. The description sounded like Howie Livingston, the director. What the heck was going on here?

"So you didn't know Mr. Cremshaw outside of the reviews he gave Starlight?" Keanu asked.

Jonathan shook his head. "In the past five years I've been here, he's reviewed the restaurant twice. Both times he gave us a measly one star. There was no reason for it either. Pure spite, I tell you. Last time he reviewed the place was about a year ago. I was so enraged when I saw the write-up in *Dining Is Divine* that I went to his room to confront him. He always stayed at Aloha Lagoon when he came to Kauai. The man was the cheapest miser you ever saw. He made Ebenezer Scrooge look generous. He never tipped my servers and was always sniffing around, looking for free food. You'd think he was destitute or something."

He paused in an obvious attempt to get his emotions under control. Jonathan's light-colored complexion had turned a bright shade of crimson. "Do you know what Cremshaw did then? He told me he'd print a retraction if we furnished all his meals for free the entire week of his stay. Can you believe the gall?"

Keanu looked at me. "Gee, that sounds familiar."

"I was so annoyed that I pushed him." Jonathan produced a white silk handkerchief from his lapel pocket and dabbed at his forehead with it. "It's not like I decked the guy, honest. Unfortunately, Randolph lost his balance and hit his head on the coffee table. He threatened to sue me and the entire resort. He ended up getting his food free for the week so that everything would stay on a hush-hush level. What a lowlife."

Keanu's expression was grim. "He sounds like he was a real piece of work."

"No doubt about it. So, who delivered the food to him from the Loco Moco the other day?" Jeff asked. "Was it you or your father?"

I pointed to myself. "That would be me."

Jonathan stared at me, his gray eyes wide with alarm. "You poor thing. So now he's got you involved too."

A muscle ticked in Keanu's jaw. "Not if I can help it. Jonathan, I would appreciate it if you could keep this under wraps. Carrie doesn't need the aggravation of fingers pointed at her wherever she goes."

Jonathan held a hand up. "Keanu, I would never say anything, rest assured. I know how important the Loco Moco is to you."

Keanu leaned across the table. "There are more important things than the Loco Moco." He cut his eyes to me, and the heat rose through my face.

We paused the conversation as the waiter returned with coffee for Keanu and me. "Would either of you care for dessert?" he asked.

Keanu looked at me questioningly, but I shook my head. "No, thank you."

"We'll take the check when you have a moment," Keanu

said. The man bowed slightly and then hurried away.

As I added creamer to my cup, a lightbulb clicked on in my head. "Jonathan, what kind of coffee is this?"

Jonathan puffed out his chest. "Kona, of course. The best and most expensive brand in the world. It's grown on the Big Island, you know."

How interesting. What if Starlight had delivered coffee to Randolph the same morning I did? Poncho had mentioned that Randolph might drink up to ten cups a day. Could someone at the restaurant have doctored up a special batch for the much-hated food critic?

Jonathan watched me intently as I sipped at the drink and then made the appropriate noises he expected. "Oh, this is delicious. The entire meal was."

He flushed with pleasure and rose to his feet. "I'm always so happy to hear that. Well, if there's nothing else, I need to have a word with the chef." He spotted our waiter heading toward us with the check and held up a hand. "No need, Nick. This one's on the house."

Nick nodded in acknowledgment and then began to clear away our plates.

Keanu stood as well. "I can't let you do that, Jonathan."

"I *insist*." Jonathan gave me a slightly forced smile and then shook Keanu's hand again. "You two enjoy the rest of your evening."

I watched him head in the direction of the kitchen while Keanu laid down two twenties for a tip. He then slipped his hand through mine as we left the restaurant.

"That entire conversation left me a bit uncomfortable," I confessed.

"Tell me about it," he muttered. "Jonathan's never comped a meal for me before, and I certainly wouldn't expect him to. It almost felt like a bribe—as if he wanted me to forget all about our conversation."

"That thought crossed my mind too."

He opened the Jeep door for me. "Let's head over to see Coral. This ought to be good for a few laughs."

I was dreading the experience but hoped that I might have a chance to ask her about the Facebook picture with

Randolph "Who's working at the restaurant tonight?"

"Vivian and Anna are there, and Poncho will close up. It's his scheduled night anyway." He slipped an arm around my waist. "It's probably more appropriate if you wait in the car while I talk to Coral. I know you wanted to ask her about the picture with Cremshaw but—"

"Don't worry about it," I assured him. "Maybe I can pay her a separate visit." She'd probably slam the door in my face, but hey, I'd give it my best shot. Keanu was right. This was a private matter between an employee and manager, and I didn't need to be privy to it.

"After Coral's out of the way, I want to enjoy the rest of the evening with my lady and forget about this entire mess for a while. Any objections?"

I beamed. "None whatsoever."

CHAPTER TWELVE

———

Coral's home was located on the outskirts of town at 22 Wiki Lane, in the opposite direction of my apartment. It took us about fifteen minutes from the resort to arrive at the small one-story home with beige vinyl siding and a metal fence surrounding the house.

"Good luck. I hope you can catch her alone." If the rest of her family was home, that would make things even more awkward for Coral and Keanu.

Keanu leaned over to kiss me. "She should have thought of that before stealing from *my* parents. I've never taken anything that didn't belong to me. Well, wait. There was that time when I was five years old and stole a candy bar from a convenience store. When my mother saw me with it in the backseat of the car, she drove right back and forced me to apologize to the owner." He chuckled at the memory. "I'll never forget it. I cried and begged to go home. But parents need to discipline their kids, right?"

I said nothing and silently recalled the awful time my mother had discovered a pack of cigarettes in my dresser drawer when I was sixteen and forced me to eat one. "Do they taste good now?" she had taunted me.

In tune as always, Keanu surmised that something was wrong. "Maybe I shouldn't have said that."

I managed a smile for him. "Didn't you once tell me that someone took money from Kara's store as well?"

He nodded, his expression grim. "Someone broke in one night and stole all the cash out of her register. Kara was going through chemo at the time, and it certainly didn't help her condition any. Shortly afterward Hale ended up evicting her." He pressed his lips together in obvious contempt. "I know there are people forced to steal because they have nothing, but it's hard for me to be sympathetic to ones like Coral."

I watched as he slammed the door and walked up the driveway with powerful strides toward the house. Before her death, Kara had owned a small clothing boutique situated in our former boss's shopping mall in Oahu. She'd been evicted when she couldn't pay her rent, and Keanu had never gotten over Hale's shabby treatment of his sister. This situation with Coral wasn't just about money for Keanu or his parents. It was a matter of trust and integrity. Keanu hated anything that smacked of dishonesty.

If Kara had lived, I felt certain we would have been good friends. From what Keanu had told me about his sister, we liked a lot of the same things—theater, television shows, cats. Maybe she even would have become like a sister to me—the sister Penny never was. Deep down, I still craved that family bond and probably always would.

I continued to sit there, lost in my own thoughts. After a few minutes, I noticed Keanu approaching my side of the vehicle. "Done already?"

"Not quite." He opened the car door for me. "Coral would like to see you and apologize for something that she did."

I winced. "Keanu, it's not necessary. I—"

"It *is* necessary." He took my hand and escorted me up the driveway and down a sidewalk that led to a screen door. "Coral admitted that she was responsible for the Tabasco sauce stunt. I told her you were in the car, and she said she'd like to apologize in person."

I glanced at him with a fair amount of doubt. Keanu probably told Coral that it would be in her best interest to apologize if she wanted his family to go easy on her regarding the stolen money. "Fine. Let's get it over with."

Keanu led the way to a small living room off a narrow hallway where a tabby cat dozed peacefully on the arm of a light blue velvet love seat. Coral was sitting in a matching chair across from it, staring down at the wooden floor. She looked up at me and then back down at the floor again.

"Hi, Coral," I greeted her.

Coral wasted no time with her apology, but still stared at the floor. "I'm sorry about the sauce. It was a stupid thing to do." She eyed Keanu. "But I don't know why you're asking me about the missing money from the register. I had nothing to do with that."

I felt certain that she had only admitted to the ketchup incident because it was the lesser of two evils. No one wanted to be accused of stealing.

Keanu settled back in the love seat and crossed his right foot over his left knee. The cat quickly made its way into his ready-made lap. "Suppose you start by telling me the truth."

Her nostrils flared. "I *am* telling you the truth."

Keanu's face was unreadable as he spoke in a calm demeanor. "Coral, if you needed money, why didn't you ask me or my father? We could have given you an advance on your salary."

"I told you I didn't do it." Coral gave me a sordid glance. "Maybe it was your girlfriend here."

Although sorely tempted, I chose not to pass a remark. There was no reason for me to defend myself to her.

"Don't drag Carrie into this," Keanu warned. "We have footage from a security camera that was recently installed. There was a picture of you from last night placing cash into your pockets."

Coral's cheeks flushed bright red, and she didn't answer.

"Why did you take the money?" Keanu asked.

Coral's bottom lip trembled, and tears started to roll down her cheeks. "Because I have tuition bills I can't afford to pay on my salary."

"Couldn't you get a student loan?" I asked.

She shot me a dirty look. "I only qualify for a certain amount, and there wasn't a bank willing to give me the rest. Don't pretend like you understand because that's bull. I'm sure Keanu takes care of everything *you* need."

My temper flared, and this time I didn't attempt to control it. The words *gold digger* were still fresh in my brain. "Keanu's family may be wealthy, but that doesn't mean I'm getting money from him. I have bills to pay, just like you do."

She put a hand on the side of her face, as if attempting to

block me from her line of vision. "I would have paid you back someday, Keanu."

He sighed heavily. "Coral, we won't press charges as long as you're honest with me about everything."

She removed the hand and hiccupped back a small sob. "All right. What else do you want to know?"

Keanu continued to pet the cat, which looked like he had no intention of ever moving from his lap. "First off, why did you fill the ketchup containers with hot sauce? Was it just to get Carrie into trouble, or was there another reason?"

Coral shifted in her seat. "It was the morning that he—the food critic—came in. I was alone with Poncho first thing, and he was so busy that he didn't even notice what I was doing." She paused for breath. "I removed two containers from Carrie's station but didn't have time to bring the new ones out before—" Coral paused.

Her voice sent an Arctic chill through me. "Before what? Why would you do this to me?" I'd always tried to be nice to the girl.

Coral narrowed her eyes. "I was jealous of you. You have everything that I want. Did you know that I tried out for a part at the Hana Hou as well? That was the first time I've ever auditioned for anything, and it was hard for me. I'm a theater major too. You probably get every role you want, have a great family, and you also have—" She looked at Keanu but didn't finish the sentence.

It was amazing that someone who didn't even know me could think my life was perfect. "You're right. I do have a good life. But it hasn't always been like that."

Coral's expression was puzzled. "What do you mean?"

"Forget about me. Let's talk about you." I wasn't about to discuss my family with Coral. I didn't enjoy talking about them with anyone, including Keanu, but Coral was still a virtual stranger in many ways. Given everything that had already happened, I doubted the girl could be trusted. Sure, she had apologized, but that didn't matter. "Are your parents married?"

Keanu continued to pet the cat in silence, happy to let me conduct my own line of questioning.

She reached for a tissue on the coffee table. "No. My

mother is all that I have, and she's wonderful. Keanu, please don't tell her about this. She'd freak."

"If you cooperate," Keanu said, "and pay back the money, no one will ever hear about it. I give you my word."

Curiosity reigned over my mouth. "I have a question. What's your relationship to Randolph Cremshaw?"

Coral appeared startled, almost as if I'd dared ask how her love life was. "The food critic who died? What makes you think I had a relationship with *him*?"

"Because I saw a picture on Facebook of the two of you together. It was taken a few years ago."

She twisted the tissue between her hands and said nothing.

I decided to try another tactic. "Was he a relative?"

Her dark eyes met mine, and she blew out a long sigh. "You could say that. He was my father."

CHAPTER THIRTEEN

———

Keanu eyed Coral suspiciously. "Was that another reason you fooled with the ketchup containers? Because you knew that your father was coming in?"

Coral was shocked. "No! I had no idea he was coming to the Loco Moco that day, honest. When I spotted him at the restaurant, shortly after Carrie got there, I ran out the patio door toward the beach because I didn't *want* to see him. I forgot about the containers until I learned what happened." She bit into her lower lip. "Like I said before, I wanted to get you into trouble. When I found out dear old Dad ate the hot sauce, I considered it a bonus."

Keanu raked a hand through his hair. "Well, at least we've solved one mystery."

This was disturbing. Coral had no regrets about what she'd done to me or her father. I knew nothing about her life and was careful not to pass judgment. Perhaps killing her with kindness was the way to go. "I'm sorry for your loss."

She pressed her lips together in a stubborn manner. "Don't be. He never acted like a father to me. When my mother told him she was pregnant, he didn't want anything to do with either one of us. Oh, he'd send her a check occasionally, but that was all. He never gave me anything, including his love. The last time he came to the house was when I was sixteen. My mother raised me, not *him*." Her next statement shocked me. "I'm glad he's dead."

I shivered at the words. "You don't mean that."

Coral's face was pinched tight with anger. "Yes, I do! He wouldn't even give me any money for college. My mother can barely make ends meet, but do you think he'd offer to lend a hand? He's got plenty of money. Instead he lets that trampy wife of his have it all."

Okay, now we were getting somewhere. Coral was not a fan of Belinda's. "How do you get along with your stepmother?"

Coral clenched her fists at her side. "I don't. They've only been married a couple of years. I've never actually met her, and don't care to."

"How often did your father come to Hawaii?" I asked. "He used to live here, right?"

"He grew up in Honolulu, but he spent some time in Kauai after graduation and always comes back at least once a year for a visit. Of course, it has nothing to do with me living here." Her lower lip trembled. "When Dad started making a name for himself in the food business, he decided that he was better suited to an atmosphere like Los Angeles, so he moved there. That's where he met—her. *Belinda*." Coral almost spat the name out. "If you want to know the person who killed him, look no further than dear old stepmommy. I'd stake my life on it."

Keanu and I exchanged glances. "Why would she want to kill your father?" he asked.

Coral's laugh was hollow. "Isn't it obvious? Money, of course. I have to go see some dopey detective at the police station tomorrow, thanks to her. Apparently when he questioned her this morning, she gave him my name, so he knows of my existence."

"But Belinda was a model. She must have made a ton of money at her profession," I said, remembering Keanu's words from earlier.

Coral furrowed her brow. "She lost a lot of dough through bad investments, and now she's too old to get any really good gigs. Belinda's just a washed-up has-been whose career was tainted by scandal."

"What kind of scandal?" Keanu asked.

Coral snickered. "She lusts after men—younger men, that is. Guys about your age. She met Dad one night when he was reviewing a restaurant in Hollywood a few years ago. Belinda must have decided he'd make a great meal ticket. Since then there's rumors she's had affairs with several camera men, directors, and even my uncle. I heard from a mutual friend that my father found out and was getting ready to file for divorce."

"Did they have a prenup?" I asked.

She did a palms-up. "No idea. But I'm betting she stands to inherit money, or a life insurance policy at the very least. The will hasn't been read yet, but I'm sure Mom and I will get squat, like always."

"When was the last time you actually spoke to or saw your father?" Keanu asked.

"I called Daddy dearest a few days before he got into town. That's how I found out he was coming to the island." Her voice filled with bitterness. "I asked him to please reconsider about the money, and once again he refused. Do you know what my father told me? That I needed to do things for myself. Boy, that's rich. I'm his only child. He's my father, so isn't he supposed to help me? He always gave Mom a hard time about child support too. Finally she got so sick of the battle that she stopped asking. Do you have any idea what it feels like to know your own father never wanted you?"

My insides were hollow. Yes, I did know. It was an all-too-familiar feeling. "You've been dealt a crummy blow, Coral, but at least you have a mother who loves you unconditionally." It still made me sad at times to realize I would never have that in my life.

Keanu watched me anxiously, almost as if he was aware of the inner battle I was fighting. We'd only had one prior discussion about my parents, but he knew how much I hated to talk about my family. I tried not to let their lack of caring define who I was.

"You're right," Coral said. "I wouldn't have survived without my mother. Dad lived here with Mom for a while, you know. When he found out about me, he couldn't scurry away fast enough. He even had the nerve to leave a pile of junk down in the basement. He told my mother he'd be back for the stuff, but never took it." Her mouth quivered. "It's been sitting there collecting dust for over twenty years. I'd get rid of it, but that's all I have left of him now."

My curiosity went into overdrive. "What kind of stuff?"

"Oh, a couple of old crates with pictures and yearbooks and other useless crap from his college days. Mom said he was a notorious pack rat who never threw anything away."

My brain zoomed in on Belinda's comment from earlier today. *He's got enemies going back to his college days, maybe even before.* "I'd love to see them, if possible." Of course, it didn't mean we'd find anything, but was still worth a shot.

Coral studied me with a puzzled expression. "Why? What would you want with that old crap?"

I tried to keep my tone casual. "Sometimes you can learn a lot about a person from their past."

She continued to watch me with unbridled suspicion. "Do you think there's something in there that could lead us to his killer?"

I shrugged. "Hard to say."

Coral's eyes blazed with an intensity that unnerved me. "I already told you who killed him. Belinda."

Wow. She really did hate the woman with a passion.

"Do you know if your father invited Belinda here to join him?" Keanu asked.

"From what I heard, she flew here to plead with him to give her another chance. When he refused, she decided to kill him before the divorce was final, so she'd still be entitled to his money."

Keanu and I listened quietly to Coral's rampage. There was a chance she was telling the truth. Still, someone who had tried to get me into trouble and had also stolen money from her employers didn't earn my trust. Then again, she could've been trying to place blame on her stepmother because she resented the woman. I figured she would give Detective Ray the same information about Belinda tomorrow and would fail to mention our visit to him. It seemed a safe assumption that she wouldn't want to be indicted on an embezzlement charge.

Coral bristled at our silence. "Why don't you believe me?"

"We believe you, Coral." I was so curious to see Randolph's memorabilia that I would have told her almost anything she wanted to hear right now, just to stay on her good side. "Can we still see your father's personal items?"

She tossed her long hair behind her and rose. "Wait here." Coral left the room, and then the distinct click of her sandals hitting the stairs could be heard as she plodded on down to the basement.

"So Belinda remains at the top of the list," I whispered. "What if Coral's right and she did kill him to prevent the divorce? I wish we could have a look at his will."

"I wouldn't rule Coral out either," Keanu said in a low voice.

"I know." I couldn't fathom doing something so horrible to your own flesh and blood. Then again, perhaps I didn't want to.

Before we could resume our conversation, Coral's footsteps sounded and she reappeared with two plastic gray crates in her hands. Keanu sprang forward to relieve her of them. He set the crates down on the coffee table in front of us. I eyeballed them quickly, trying not to be too obvious about my interest. Unfortunately, they looked like useless items. There were textbooks, old college newspapers, and even a few playbills that I longed to browse. "Was your father a theater major, like yourself?"

She shook her head. "I think he started out doing some reviews for his college newspaper. He always loved to write. Eventually he figured there was more money in food than theater."

Interesting. Jeff had mentioned that they all went to school together. Perhaps I could pick up on something by looking through the papers, like an old girlfriend who was out for revenge. And what about Coral's mother?

Coral picked up a silver-framed photograph of her father at his graduation ceremony and studied it. "Look at this. Would you believe that the picture on Facebook is the only one that I have of us together? The only photo I ever *will* have." She ran a hand across her eyes.

Although I was still angry about what Coral had done to me, I could relate to her plight. There was no reason to make comparisons, but at least she was one up on me. I had no photos of my father at all. I probably wouldn't recognize him if he walked down the same street as me.

Keanu lifted out an old college newspaper. "Coral, would you mind if we looked through these? We can do it now, as long as you don't mind us staying for a while."

She glanced at the wall clock nervously. "My mother is due home any minute."

This might work to our advantage. If Coral was anxious to get rid of us before her mother arrived, she might not mind us taking the items with us. Of course, Keanu could always play his trump card regarding the theft if needed, but I didn't think she'd refuse.

"Maybe someone had a grudge against him," Keanu said. "It might have been going on for years."

Coral's nostrils flared. "I already told you who killed him. My stepmother."

She was starting to get agitated, and I didn't want to push our luck. I tried desperately to think of a diversion. "Did you know I was the one to find your father?"

Her face paled. "*You*? You brought him the food the other day? I thought maybe Poncho had gone."

"No." I wasn't going to get into graphic details about what her father had looked like in his final hour but thought she should know that I was being scrutinized as well. After all, it was partially her fault because of the ketchup mix-up. "I've been questioned by the police too. Even if you're positive Belinda had a hand in this, the police will want proof. We'd like to help find some, if it exists."

"I'm not looking forward to speaking to that cop." Coral glanced anxiously at Keanu. "You're sure you didn't tell the police about the—you know—money? You can take the crates as long as you bring them back and promise you won't tell my mother what I did."

Keanu's manner was calm. "I already gave you my word. If you sign a paper that I draw up and agree to pay back the money over time, we won't press charges. But you do realize we can't have you working there anymore."

Coral's lower lip trembled. "Yes, I understand."

As we rose to our feet, I turned to address Coral again. "I forgot to ask you about your uncle Richard."

She narrowed her eyes. "Dad's little brother? Yeah, another relative who's fond of keeping in touch. *Not.* He's too busy hanging out with his sister-in-law, if you get my drift."

"Richard knows you and your mother live here?" I asked.

"Of course," she said. "I'm the black sheep of the family. They all know of my presence but choose to avoid me."

"Were Richard and your father close?" Too late, I realized this was a stupid question. If Belinda and Richard were fooling around, the brothers were most likely not the most loving of siblings.

She made a face. "Mom said they were years ago, during college. Given everything that's happened with Belinda, I doubt it now."

Keanu picked up both crates, and I ran to hold the front door open for him. As I was about to join him, Coral held out a hand for me to shake. Surprised, I took it.

"I lied," she whispered.

For a moment, I wondered if she was referring to her father's murder. "About what?"

Tears gathered in her eyes. "I *am* sorry he's dead. Does that even make any sense? He was a rotten father, but I still wanted his approval and his love. I'll never have either one now."

"It makes perfect sense," I assured her. "It hurts, but you can't let this consume you. There will be plenty of other people in your lifetime to love and care about you." I would have loved the opportunity to speak with her mother, but this might not be the best time. "How's your mom handling his death?"

She smiled. "Mom's tough. She got over his treatment of her long ago. It takes a special kind of person to shake off their past like that."

I liked to think that this referred to me as well. There was no point in dwelling on the past anymore, but it would always remain a part of me. At least Coral had known the conventional bedtime story, visits to the circus, someone to teach her to ride a bike or go to the movies with. I'd had none of these. When I came to Hawaii, I'd broken off all contact with my family back in Vermont. I'd never make my mother love me, so what was the point of trying anymore?

My mind traveled back to one painful incident when I was about eleven and my mother and sister had gone to the movies, leaving me home alone although I'd begged to come along. To keep myself from crying, I'd spent the entire evening pretending to be a famous actress giving an awards acceptance speech. No matter what happened, I'd always had my dreams. They'd sustained me through some of the darkest periods of my life, and no one could ever take them away.

Coral watched me with an odd expression as I struggled to clear my head. Why was I remembering this now? No more feeling sorry for myself. Instead, I focused my attention on the handsome man who walked toward me, a broad smile on his face. Somehow, he made the past less painful to deal with, and for that I was beyond grateful.

"You're right," I said to Coral. "It is hard to shake off the past at times. But to move forward with your life, it's also necessary."

CHAPTER FOURTEEN

———

"Check this out," Keanu said. He was reading a copy of *College Chatter*, the newspaper that Randolph had written for. "'Dining Hall Food—Even the Rats Won't Touch It,' by Randolph Cremshaw." He whistled low under his breath. "It sounds like Cremshaw's reviews haven't changed much in twenty years, huh?"

We were sitting on my couch going through the contents of the crates. Benny kept leaping from the coffee table, where we had placed them, to the arm of the couch, serving as general inspector while we sorted through the dusty papers and other paraphernalia. The papers smelled moldy, and I'd already had to wash my hands twice from the dirt. If we could learn a little about Randolph's past life it would make this well worth the inconvenience.

Keanu kissed me on the neck. "I'll play Watson to your Sherlock any day."

"You say the most romantic things," I teased, engrossed in skimming a playbill from an old theater production. "Look at the title of this show. *Destiny in December*. Interesting."

He flashed his dimple. "Sounds like a great name for a porno."

I smacked him in the arm with the playbill, and we both laughed. When I glanced down at the paper again, my jaw went slack. The play was written and directed by none other than Jeffrey Temple. I studied the rest of the names and gasped.

Keanu leaned over to get a better look. "What is it?"

"They were all in this show!" Under the Cast of Characters list I spotted Howie's name along with Richard's and Randolph's. Randolph had played a character named Frederick.

"What the heck! Do you think this could mean anything?"

He shrugged. "Jeff told you that they all went to school together, right?"

I nodded. "They hung out together."

"It may not be that unusual, Care. How long ago was this play? Jeff's what, around forty or so?"

The front page of the playbill said it was from 1995. "I get what you're saying. It probably doesn't have anything to do with Randolph's death, but I thought maybe it would help to know a little more about him." I was anxious to get out from underneath Detective Ray's scrutiny. He would be more than happy to find something that connected me to Randolph's murder. Didn't he know he should be looking at Belinda, who was most likely having an affair with Randolph's brother? And how exactly did Howie fit into this?

"Here are the bios," I said to Keanu as he wrapped both arms around my waist and pulled me close. "Listen to this. 'Jeffrey Temple, Writer and Director. Jeff is a theater major who recently appeared in the musical productions of *Godspell* and *The Fantasticks*. Upon graduation, Jeff plans to pursue theater and work in the family jewelry store, Diamonds Are Us.'"

"Gee, that's an original name." Keanu placed a kiss on my shoulder.

I giggled. "'Howard Gabriel Livingston (Abe) is a theater and communications major. *Destiny in December* marks his first theater appearance. After graduation, he hopes to go to Hollywood and take it by storm.'"

Keanu kept kissing me. "Dreams do come true, it seems."

"And here's the bio for our favorite food critic. 'Randolph Cremshaw (Frederick) is a business major with a minor in culinary arts. He is also features editor for *College Chatter*. After graduation, Randolph plans to review theater productions for a local newspaper.'"

Keanu's hot breath was on my neck and his lips moved lower, making it difficult for me to concentrate. My heart started to pound against the wall of my chest.

"Go on," Keanu murmured as his hands reached under my shirt. "I'm getting excited listening to all this talk about culinary. It must be the restaurateur in me."

I laughed, but desire started to flood through my body. I put the playbill down and threw my arms around him as we kissed passionately. He gently lowered me onto the couch, where we continued the embrace for several minutes. I pushed the shirt over his head while he went to work on mine. At that moment, a vision of Terry glaring at me entered my mind, and I froze in panic.

In tune to my body as always, Keanu stopped kissing me immediately. "Carrie, I'm starting to get a complex here."

When I didn't answer, Keanu heaved a sigh and lifted his body off mine. I continued to lie there, convinced something must be wrong with me. I'd had no problem saying yes to a womanizer such as Brad, but now that I was with a wonderful guy who treated me like a queen, I shut down whenever he wanted to take our relationship to the next level. I didn't know how to explain my behavior and for the first time feared I might end up losing him over this.

I raised myself up and touched his arm lightly. To my relief, he didn't pull away. "I'm sorry. I don't know what's wrong with me because I do want to be with you. It's just—"

He gave me a reassuring smile then got to his feet. "It's fine, Carrie. I understand."

Okay, I was tempted to ask him to explain it to me because I didn't understand. Before I could say anything further, he picked his car keys up off the coffee table and gave me a quick kiss on the cheek. "I'm going to give you some space."

Some space. A veiled expression for a breakup. Panic set in. "Please don't leave like this."

He placed his hands on my shoulders. "Carrie, I'm not breaking up with you. I care too much about you to do that. In fact—" He hesitated, as if grasping for the right words. "There's something I've wanted to say to you for a while. To be honest, I wasn't sure if you could handle it, but I can't wait any longer."

Oh God. Dread as heavy as a mountain settled in the pit of my stomach. "It's your father, isn't it? He said he'd disinherit you unless you broke up with me."

He stared at me in disbelief. "Wow. That imagination of yours is something else. No, it's not like that at all. My parents will never dictate who's in my life. We've been over this already."

It was times like this when I wanted to smack myself in the head. I'd started to think of myself as self-assured, confident, and ready to handle anything life threw at me, but insecurity had become my best friend lately. "You're right. I don't know what's wrong with—"

"I love you, Carrie."

Keanu's words stopped me cold. He reached up a hand to stroke my cheek, and our eyes met. As always I was mesmerized by the bright blue gaze of his. I'd dreamed of hearing those three little words for a long time. Now that he'd said them, I wasn't sure if I could handle the repercussions.

"You *love* me?" I managed to squeak out.

Keanu nodded and kissed me softly on the mouth while I continued to stare at him, in some sort of a trance. "It's not something I just discovered tonight. I've known for quite a while but was afraid to tell you."

"Why?" My voice cracked with emotion.

He ran a hand through my hair. "Because of this. I didn't know if it would freak you out. And I'm not telling you so that you'll sleep with me. I don't play games like that." He grinned and flashed his perfect white teeth. "Even though you won't talk about it, I know you have some emotional scars that cut pretty deep. You might not be ready for this, and that's okay. I'm a patient man and not going anywhere. But I honestly think that the murder and musical are stressing you out. When the show is done, we'll see where things lead, okay?"

In frustration, I shook my head. "I don't want to break up. There's—"

"Whoa." Keanu put a finger on my lips. "We're not breaking up. I just told you that I loved you, silly girl. Take a few days to think about everything, okay? Sort out your feelings for me."

"There's nothing to sort out," I insisted. "I—uh—care about you very much."

Oh my God. I winced at the words. Every time I opened my mouth I managed to stick my entire foot inside. What was the matter with me? *I care about you.* I remembered Tad's mocking words. This was real life, not acting in a play. Keanu deserved so much more than I was able to give right now.

If Keanu was upset by my statement, he had the good grace not to show it. "I'll see you at the café in the morning." He kissed me again, and wove his hands through my hair. "Get some sleep, and remember that I love you."

After the door closed behind him, I sat down numbly on the couch and placed my face in my hands. Maybe Keanu was right. I had to take some time to figure things out before everything came crashing down around me.

A furry face rubbed against my hand. Benny sat next to me on the couch, purring away with the intensity of a car's engine. When I reached out a hand to pet him, he jumped onto the coffee table and sat there like a statue, staring down his nose at me with an expression that said I might be a moron.

"You're right." Benny rewarded me by turning his back to me and lifting his tail in salute. "I *am* a dope. I've finally found a wonderful man that really loves me, and all I keep doing is trying to push him away."

Perhaps my biggest fear was giving my heart away. I hadn't told Keanu this—actually no one knew—but in all of my twenty-five years on this earth, no one had ever told me that they loved me before. My mother had certainly never spoken those words to me, nor had my sister. If my father said them, I didn't have any recollection of it. Brad had never said he loved me. Instead, he'd use charming phrases such as "you rock" or "you're beautifully awesome, babe." I'd waited a long time for someone to care about me. Now that the moment had finally happened, I had no idea how to handle it.

Benny stuck his nose inside one of the crates, sniffing around, and then started to rub his head against the dusty papers inside. Apparently, he liked the feel of grunge against his fur.

"Hey." I pulled him onto my lap, and he meowed plaintively. I needed a good cry and wanted comfort, but Benny was having none of it. He jumped back onto the coffee table and pawed at one of the college newspapers. I noticed three words underneath the headline on the front page of *College Chatter—by Randolph Cremshaw*. It wasn't the issue Keanu had been reading earlier. I lifted it out, intrigued by what other words of wisdom Randolph had penned. The issue was from 1995. I'd only been three years old at the time.

"College Student Still Missing and Presumed Dead," read the headline.

After a month long search, twenty-two-year-old Sean Tyler is still missing and presumed dead. His family says they are optimistic that Sean is still alive and are holding out hope for his safe return. They are asking for everyone's prayers.

Sean, an economics major, was last seen retiring to his dorm room after dinner on Wednesday, May 10. His girlfriend, Wendy Ritzer, reported him missing the next day, saying that they were supposed to have breakfast together, but he never showed.

If anyone has information, please contact...

Ritzer. Why was the name familiar? My eyes traveled back to the playbill in the crate, and I searched under "Cast of Characters" again. *Bingo.* Wendy had played the character of Jessica. She was in nearly every scene listed, so I presumed she must have been a lead in the show.

Could this just be a weird coincidence? I sat there, lost in thought, holding the playbill in my hand while Benny continued to sleep contentedly in my lap. When I looked at the date of the show, my heart skipped a beat.

May 10, 1995.

CHAPTER FIFTEEN

The crowd at the Loco Moco was almost back to normal the next day. Monday meant new vacationers had arrived at Aloha Lagoon. Hopefully not too many had heard about the unfortunate incident with Randolph yet.

Vivian and I were busy running our tails off all morning since we were the only two servers on duty. The all-too-familiar *Help Wanted* sign adorned the front door of the café by the lobby entrance. Now that we were short a server again, Vivian was already grumbling about working more hours.

"We can never keep help here," she complained. "It looks like you and I are destined to be the only two long-term servers, kiddo."

I put together some silverware packets as she talked, but she might as well have been speaking a foreign language. Keanu had been upstairs in the office all morning. I had started to go up once when there was a brief lull in the crowd but heard him talking on the phone with a supplier and didn't want to interrupt. Although he had assured me all was okay, I remained worried that something had shifted in our relationship last night. I wanted to invite him over for dinner so that we could talk. I needed to put everything out on the table and let him know my concerns.

"Are you listening to me?" Vivian stood in front of me, hands on her hips.

"Sorry." I sighed. "My mind is on other things today."

She grabbed two coffee cups from the cabinet behind me and started to fill them from the full pot on the double-burner machine. "Keanu's acting odd today too. What's going on with you guys?"

Cripes. The Loco Moco was like the town grapevine

some days. I didn't want to get into this now, especially with customers waiting. "Nothing. Between the show and Randolph's murder, I just have a lot going on."

She patted my arm. "I can't wait to see *Little Women* this weekend. I already told Sybil she'd better not call in sick Friday night."

"Carrie!" Poncho shouted from the kitchen. "Your order's up."

I pushed through the double swinging doors and grabbed the two plates Poncho had placed on the counter. One dish was pineapple pancakes with coconut syrup while the other contained Portuguese sausage, eggs, and rice, one of our most popular breakfast entrees. Many of Aloha Lagoon guests enjoyed eating foods with an ethnic flavor to them.

Poncho waved his spatula in the air. "It is after twelve, and I am still taking breakfast orders. Why did you not cut people off an hour ago, like you are supposed to?"

Heat rose through my face. "I'm sorry, Poncho. I guess I wasn't thinking."

He eyed me shrewdly. "You are not the only one." He pointed his spatula toward the ceiling and lowered his voice. "Did you two have a fight?"

Egads. No one would let up. "We're fine."

Poncho's face twisted into a frown. "You are a bad liar, *ho'aloha.*"

Touché. Instead of responding, I headed out the swinging doors and placed the plates down in front of a couple whose eyes lit up when they saw their food. "Let me know if you need anything else."

"Waitress," a man called.

"Be right there." I grabbed a packet of silverware and a menu from behind the counter and approached the table where the summons had come from. A lone man sat there, texting on his phone, but looked up as I approached, and our eyes met. It was Richard Cremshaw.

His pretentious smile turned upside down. "You! I thought you were Ron Howard's assistant."

Of all the worse luck. *Just pretend you don't remember*

him. "This isn't my station, sir. I'll have another waitress take your order right away."

He reached out a hand and grabbed my wrist in a firm grip. "Wait a minute. That story was all bologna. I knew it was when Belinda gave me the details. Who are you really? And why were you at the Hana Hou?"

His fingers tightened around my arm, and I flinched. "Let go of me."

"Answer me first."

"Get your hands off her now."

The voice was quiet but menacing—not a tone I heard often from Keanu. He was standing behind me, hands on hips, and lips compressed tightly together as he glared at Richard.

"Cripes, do you two travel together all the time?" Richard asked. "Don't worry, fella. I'm not interested in your babe. We're just having a little talk, so you can go back to washing dishes in the kitchen."

Keanu's nostrils flared. "Yes, she is my girlfriend. She's also an employee here, and I happen to be one of the owners of the Loco Moco. No one's going to treat any of my staff like this, so if you want to keep that hand, remove it from her arm, or I'll remove yours from *your* arm."

Richard glowered for a second then reluctantly did as he was told. He rose to his feet and looked from me to Keanu. "What the hell are you two really up to? Oh wait. I get it. You're afraid Belinda's going to sue this dump. That's why you made up the bogus story about Ron Howard that she was stupid enough to fall for."

"There's no proof the Loco Moco is responsible for your brother's death." Keanu folded his arms across his chest. "From what we understand, there were several people with motives to kill him."

"Like you." I brought my hand to my mouth. *Holy cow.* I couldn't believe I'd let that slip out.

Richard's eyes shot angry sparks at me. "How dare you."

I plodded on. "You had the biggest motive of anyone. There's rumors that you and Belinda have been carrying on and that you're also contesting a will from your parents which left everything to Randolph."

Richard sucked in a sharp breath. 'You should really stop reading the *National Enquirer*. But that's probably all a tart like you can afford on your salary."

Storm clouds brewed in Keanu's eyes, and he stepped around me, putting his face up against Richard's. "Get the hell out of here."

I placed a hand on Keanu's arm. "Wait." This was perhaps the only chance we might have to question Richard, who glared at us as I examined his sneering face. "Okay. Let's assume that we're all innocent here. Who else had a motive for wanting your brother dead?"

He shrugged. "That's easy. His ex-girlfriend and mother of his only child, Sefina Palu. Randy left her with nothing, and she's been looking to get even for a long time."

I exchanged glances with Keanu. Richard was still tops on my suspect list, but I had to admit that the case against Sefina looked pretty good too. Maybe Coral had been lying. Coral could only surmise that she and her mother had been cut out of Randy's will since it hadn't been read yet. There was no way she knew the contents—or did she? "Do you have an alibi for the morning your brother was killed?"

Richard's face was crimson, and his hands shook with apparent rage. "Who the hell are you, Kauai's version of Nancy Drew? I don't have to explain anything to you, sweetie."

We were starting to attract some attention from the few diners around us. Keanu pointed to the door that led to the lobby. "Get out, and don't come back. Ever."

"You're refusing to serve me?" Richard raised his eyebrows.

"I reserve the right to refuse service to anyone," Keanu said quietly. "It's stated on our menu."

Richard attempted to hold back a laugh as his eyes fixed on me again. "Have fun with Miss Drew here. And I'm glad you won't serve me. When Belinda owns the place and demotes you to busboy, you'll be singing a different tune."

He strode angrily toward the exit, and Keanu started to follow, but I clung to his arm. "Let him go. That man's not worth the trouble."

Keanu turned to face me. The anger had died from his

eyes and been replaced with concern. "You okay?" he asked softly.

I nodded. The awkwardness from last night had returned, and we stood staring at each other in silence. A sudden lump in my throat made talking difficult.

Keanu smiled reassuringly at me as his gaze traveled to my lips. "I've got some work to finish upstairs. I'll check back with you later." With that, he turned and went into the kitchen.

After standing there dumbly for a moment, I decided to follow him upstairs. I had to make Keanu understand why I'd acted the way I did last night. When I entered the kitchen, my phone started to vibrate from my pocket. I pulled it out and saw Jeff's name.

What the heck? I fervently hoped he didn't want to hold a rehearsal tonight because I needed to straighten things out with Keanu first. I hurried into the employees' room with my phone and ignored Poncho's quizzical look as I rushed past him. "Hi, Jeff. What's up?"

"Hey, Carrie." His voice sounded terse. "Can you stop by the theater about one o'clock today?"

Intuition warned me that this was not good news. Although rare, I'd heard of people being cut in the middle of a theater performance before. There was always an eager understudy waiting in the background to take over. Tad had casually mentioned Jeff had done this during a show last season. Of course, that girl showed up drunk for rehearsal, but regardless, it had happened. No one received any preferential treatment with him. He hadn't attempted to sugarcoat how awful he thought my performance was on Saturday either.

"Why, what's the matter?" I tried to keep the uneasiness out of my voice.

He paused before answering. "I'd rather get into this when you get here. It won't take long."

"But I'm working." I wanted to prolong the inevitable as long as possible.

"Maybe you can take your lunch break then? See you soon."

He clicked off before I had a chance to respond. I stood there, staring at the phone, and felt tears well up in the recesses of my eyes. *What else could go wrong?* I sat down on the bench, put my head in my hands, and started to weep silently. Someone touched my arm, and I jumped.

Keanu was standing there, staring down at me with a perplexed look on his face. I was so distracted that I hadn't even heard him come down the stairs. The tears rolled down my cheeks as he sat down on the bench and reached for my hand.

"Care, what's wrong? Did Cremshaw come back?" His expression grew dark with worry.

"It's not him. I…uh." As I stared into his face, memories of what had occurred last night overwhelmed my brain, and everything came to a sudden head. Still weeping, I collapsed into his strong arms. He stroked my hair and held me tightly against his chest.

"Shh." His lips were by my ear. "I told you we were okay. Don't be upset."

Relief washed over me to hear those words. Of course Keanu was more important than any old show, but Jeff's call had still upset me. "I was afraid that I'd hurt you last night, and that's the last thing I ever want to do." I hiccupped back a sob. "Jeff wants to see me at the theater at one o'clock."

His body tensed against mine. "Did he tell you why?"

I shook my head. "He didn't have to. I think he's going to cut me from the show."

Keanu's jaw dropped. "Why? You were terrific, babe. I can't believe he'd be that stupid."

I smiled up at him and tried to get my emotions in check. "Thanks for that. At least I still have you."

Keanu wiped away the rest of my tears with the pad of his thumb and kissed me lightly. "You'll always have me. I'm not going anywhere. Would you like me to drive you over?"

"Excuse me." Poncho was standing in the doorway, spatula still in hand. "Keanu, I hate to interrupt, but remember that the produce man is coming at one, and he specifically asked for you. Is there another board meeting this afternoon too?"

Keanu muttered a four-letter word under his breath. "To hell with that meeting, and I can cancel Earl. It's no big deal."

"No." I reached for a tissue in my apron pocket. "Don't worry. I'll figure out something."

Poncho pointed in the direction of the café. "Tad is out front with the linen order for today. He is busy chatting it up with Vivian. Maybe he could give you a lift."

"Oh!" I wiped at my eyes. "Poncho, will you ask him to wait for me?"

He nodded and after a sobering look at both me and Keanu, turned on his heel and went back into the kitchen. Keanu sat there with his arm around my waist, patiently waiting for me to compose myself.

Get a grip, Care. It's just a show. "I didn't even ask, but is it okay if I leave for a little while? Sybil should be here soon. I doubt I'll be gone more than an hour."

"Sure, it's okay. I'll cover until she gets here." He hesitated for a moment. "Do you have plans for tonight?"

It was the opportunity I'd been waiting for, and my mouth began to work overtime. "I want to be with you. There are some things that I need to tell you. It might help you understand why last night I—"

Keanu put a finger to my lips. "Okay. We'll talk about it later. I'll stop by your place after my meeting, whenever that gets done. If I beat you there, Benny and I will hang out and watch a movie together. Maybe even a chick flick." He flashed me a teasing grin.

I had given Keanu a key to my apartment about a month ago, and he'd done likewise. It wasn't really necessary since I didn't own a car and couldn't get to his place unless he drove me. Still, it was a nice gesture on his part and wonderful to know we were in a comfortable stage in our relationship.

He rubbed his face against my hair. "How about I bring some takeout with me? What would you like?"

"I'm not sure that I'll have much of an appetite," I said honestly. Right now I only cared about two things—being with Keanu and getting through this meeting with Jeff in a somewhat composed manner. I'd be damned to let the man see me cry. "It doesn't matter what we eat. All I need is you."

He flashed his adorable dimple at me. "Okay. That request sounds easy enough for me to fulfill. Good luck, sweetheart. No matter what happens, I'm here for you."

My heart overfilled as I gazed back at him. *He really is*

all mine. I opened my mouth to say those three little words, but again they refused to come out. In frustration, I grabbed my purse from the nearby locker. "I'll see you tonight."

"Text me after you talk to him," Keanu said. "This way I'll know when I should come over and beat the crap out of him."

"Maybe I'll take you up on that," I teased.

***

Tad pulled his white convertible into a parking spot by the back door of the Hana Hou Theater, and I glanced around uneasily. There were only two other cars in the entire lot—Jeff's silver Ford Fiesta and a black BMW.

"What's up with the BMW?" Tad frowned and lifted his sunglasses to have a better look at the car. "I think that's a rental."

"Maybe it belongs to the business manager. Didn't she mention the other day that her car was in an accident?" *Great.* I'd hoped that Jeff would be the only one present. The situation was bad enough without having an audience.

"Do you want me to come inside with you, love?"

I shook my head. "Thanks anyway. It would be great if you could wait and bring me back to the Loco Moco, if you're not on a tight schedule for deliveries, that is. I'll reimburse you for the gas."

He waved a hand impatiently. "I only have a couple of more runs this afternoon, so take your time. And I would never take money from one of my BFFs. Tell you what though. I'll let you buy me a Frappuccino from Starbucks."

"You've got a deal." I opened the car door, took some deep, calming breaths, then held up my crossed fingers. "Wish me luck."

Tad crossed his fingers as well and blew me a kiss. "You've got this, hon. Keep the faith."

CHAPTER SIXTEEN

The inside of the Hana Hou was eerily quiet and semidark, with the exception of one lone stage light. My stomach began to do somersaults. *Enough of this.* I forced myself to laugh. What was I getting so upset about? I had given it my best shot and that was what counted. There were other theaters in the area, and I wasn't about to let Jeff squelch my dreams.

With my head raised high and proud, I stepped onto the dimly lighted stage and began to walk defiantly toward Jeff's office. Muffled voices were coming from the other side of the door, and I stopped to listen.

"Why were you at the restaurant with her?" Jeff asked.

A deep, familiar male voice answered. "Temple, you know I didn't have anything to do with Randy's death."

Instinctively, I covered my mouth with my hand. Howie was in there. Why was he here if Jeff was expecting me? Had I gotten the time wrong? Confused, I glanced down at my watch and noticed it said twelve o'clock. That couldn't be right. I pulled out my phone, and the time read 12:58. My watch must have stopped again.

Maybe they had just returned from lunch? If Jeff caught me eavesdropping again, he'd really be furious. Regardless, I pressed my ear up against the door anyway.

"I didn't say that you did," Jeff responded. "But please don't tell me you're still carrying a torch for her."

"Look," Howie said. "I may have had a thing for her years ago, and yeah, I did help Belinda out the other night when she was short on cash. The truth of the matter is that she's just a washed-up model who's had way too much plastic surgery. There's no fresh or redeeming qualities about her any more. Do you know what she did last night? She came to my room and offered me a good time in exchange for a part in my next film." He chuckled. "She said it would be a night I'd never forget."

Ew. My stomach churned. So, all the rumors I'd heard about Hollywood were apparently true.

There was another moment's silence before Jeff spoke. "I see."

"No, you don't," Howie retorted. "Jeff, I don't operate that way. And you have my word that I would never do that to one of your actresses."

They were talking about Rose now. That was why Howie was there—he'd be flying Rose off to California for a part in his movie. Even though I was happy for her, my heart sank as realization set in, and I envied her with every fiber of my being. I couldn't stand it any longer. So much for prolonging my suffering—I needed to get this over with. I sucked in a deep breath and knocked on the door.

Jeff opened it immediately and smiled. "Carrie, you're right on time. Come in." He gestured toward Howie. "You remember my old buddy Howie, right? The dapper director, as he's known."

I nodded, not daring to breathe.

"Sit down." Jeff offered me a chair.

I glanced with hesitation at Howie. *Does he have to be here?* The entire experience was humiliating enough. "Um, I can wait until the both of you are done talking."

Howie shook his head. "We've been waiting for you, dear."

Despite my so-called act of confidence and assurance, nausea stirred in the pit of my stomach. I shouldn't have eaten that breakfast burrito Poncho had made me earlier. At the time it had sounded great—scrambled eggs, fried rice, and Portuguese sausage with cheddar cheese in a flour tortilla. The guacamole and sour cream probably hadn't helped either. *Just say it and get this over with.* "Rhonda will make a great Beth. I'll call her and congratulate her."

Rhonda was the understudy for both myself and Jennifer—the woman who played my sister Amy. Of course this was also good news for Lena, the understudy for Rose. "And I'll be sure to congratulate Rose too," I offered. "She deserves the opportunity."

Howie and Jeff were staring at me like I had two heads.

"Carrie," Jeff said. "You're not making any sense. What does Rhonda have to do with this?"

My cheeks were on fire. "I...uh, figured that she'd be taking over for me."

Jeff shook his head. "There's no need. Howie's willing to let you finish out the show before you go to California."

"There are no hard feelings," I babbled on. "I know my singing was terrible, and really appreciate that you gave me a chance."

Wait a second. What did he just say? "I'm going to— *where*?"

Both men roared with laughter at my reaction, and Jeff again gestured to the empty chair. "Carrie, please sit down. I don't want you to fall over before I tell you that Howie would like you to screen test for a part in his next movie."

My legs trembled like Jell-O, and I couldn't move. "You want *me*? Not Rose? But I thought—"

Jeff walked over and gently helped lower me into a chair. Once I was seated, he flopped down in the one behind his desk. "You thought I was firing you?"

My brain was a mass of jumbled confusion, and I struggled to take it all in. "This can't be real." I spoke the words more to myself.

Howie cleared his throat. "It's very real, Carrie. I'd like to have you out in Hollywood as soon as the show finishes, the weekend after next. That would give you enough time to get your affairs in order here, right?"

"What about Rose?" I asked. "Is she going too?"

Jeff and Howie exchanged a glance.

"Don't get me wrong," Howie said. "Rose is extremely talented with a lovely singing voice, but she's a bit too pretentious on stage. You're the real deal. You have a gift, Carrie. A natural, fresh quality that comes across the stage and fills the entire room. That's what I'm looking for. There's a small role for a kindergarten teacher in my next movie, which is called *Princes Can Be Charming*. Monique Danson is the lead, and you would play her sister."

My jaw almost hit the floor. "*The* Monique Danson? I love her movies!"

Howie grinned. "Now, I can't promise you anything—yet. You'd have to take a screen test when you get out there. We'll take care of your airfare and set you up in a place to stay until the test is finished. If things don't work out, at least there won't be much of a cost involved for you." He puffed out his chest a bit. "There's always a chance the project could get shelved, but that's never happened with one of *my* movies."

I continued to stare at him, in a bit of a trance. What I had fantasized about my entire life was finally coming true. *My big dream.* Since I was a little girl, I had longed to be a professional actor or singer. Even though I loved to sing, I'd finally realized I possessed zero talent for it. Sure, several members of the audience had commented on how much they had enjoyed my acting performance, but no one had ever told me before that I had actual talent. I'd always assumed that the audience was just being nice. "How long would I be there?"

"Three months at most," Howie replied. "I'll have my secretary make all the arrangements and send everything over so you can take a look at your leisure."

My voice cracked with emotion. "Thank you so much, Howie. I promise not to let you down."

Jeff laughed. "Carrie, you sound like you could use a bottle of water. I'll grab one out of the fridge. Be right back." He opened the door to his office, and his loafers could be heard tapping against the wooden stage floor.

Howie reached over to pat my hand. "This could open a lot of doors for you, Carrie. Hollywood is always looking for fresh talent."

"Thank you so much." My entire body shook. "It'll be quite a change from slinging hash at the Loco Moco."

Howie's smile faded. "Jeff told me you were the one to find Randy in his hotel room."

The memory of Randolph's dead body once again embedded itself into my brain. "Yes. There are rumors that his wife might try to sue the Loco Moco, so we've been trying to figure out who's responsible." I wasn't sure if I should say anything more about Belinda, especially if Howie was still fond of her.

Howie's mouth tightened in a firm, taut line. "It doesn't surprise me. Belinda's pretty desperate for money these days, and Randy was worth more to her dead than alive, if you get my drift."

Only too well. "Are you saying she could have done it?"

Howie shook his head. "I would never accuse someone of a crime without all the details. But the fact remains that she had a motive, and a huge one. Don't get me wrong. A lot of people wanted the man dead. Lord knows I wasn't too fond of him myself either, but I'd never have done such a thing."

An involuntary shiver went down my spine. "Do you remember a man named Sean Tyler who went to the college with you?"

He eyed me sharply. "Of course. He took off one night and was never heard from again. Where did you hear about this?"

How to get out of this one. "Uh, I enjoy following cold cases. It's a hobby of mine since I majored in criminal justice." The lies tumbled out of my mouth too freely and I was getting myself in deeper. "Jeff mentioned that he went to college with you, and I wondered if you knew Sean personally."

Howie shook his head. "Not personally. His girlfriend had the lead in a play that I was also in. Her name was Wendy Ritzer." A broad smile creased his face. "Every guy wanted to make it with her."

Real nice, Howie.

He laughed at the expression on my face. "Aw Carrie, give me a break. All of us college guys thought like that. Wendy wanted to be in the play and jumped at the chance to audition. She even had the nerve to call me last year and ask if I'd fly her out to Hollywood." He shook his head in disbelief. "Some things will never change. Her, uh, stage presence wasn't exactly what she was known for back in college."

That was obvious. "Do you know where she is now?"

"Last time we spoke, I believe Wendy said that she travels back and forth between Oahu and Kauai for work. Wendy's been married and divorced four times. Guess she thinks she might be the next Elizabeth Taylor." Howie snickered. "She recently sent me an 8-by-10 photo of herself. Let's just say that the years have not been kind to her."

If I could track the woman down, would she be willing to talk to me? What would it prove? Maybe nothing. "Sean disappeared the same night as a theater production at the college. It was a show called *Destiny in December*."

Howie's eyes widened in obvious recognition as Jeff reappeared and handed me a bottle of Evian.

"What's this about *Destiny in December*?" Jeff asked. "It's a play I wrote for my senior project in college." He sat down behind his desk, a smug look on his face. "I directed it too."

"Remember Sean Tyler?" Howie addressed Jeff but kept his eyes pinned on me. "Carrie said the night Sean disappeared was the same evening as your show. She's a big fan of cold cases."

"Really?" Jeff seemed intrigued. "You know, I do seem to remember the connection now. I don't think they ever found him. Are you giving up acting for detective work, Carrie? Howie wouldn't be pleased to hear that."

His tone was teasing, and I laughed. "It's only a hobby." I decided not to say anything else about Sean's disappearance. Howie continued to watch me, his expression curious. Okay, it was time for me to shut up now. Maybe he was afraid I'd turn out to be a troublemaker. I didn't want to do anything to jeopardize the opportunity he had afforded me.

Howie rose to his feet. "Carrie, I need to get back to my hotel. Do you need a lift?"

Although tempted, I didn't want to abandon Tad, especially after he'd been so good about bringing me here. "I have a ride outside waiting, thanks."

Howie held a business card in his hand. "I'll be in touch within the next couple of days. In the meantime, feel free to call if you have any questions. I'm headed back to California at the end of the week and might not see you until you get out there." He removed a pen from his shirt pocket and scribbled a number on the back of the card. "Call my personal cell if you need anything—anything at all."

My entire body was numb as I shook his hand. Jeff came

over and enveloped me in a warm hug, beaming from ear to ear. "This is going to look great in future programs. We'll put your picture up on the wall so we can tell everyone that you got your start right here, at the Hana Hou!"

"Thank you both so much," I said gratefully and closed the door to the office behind me, still stunned at what had taken place. My head was spinning, and I practically floated across the stage toward the exit door, feeling light as a feather.

My phone pinged with a text. I withdrew it from my pants pocket and looked down at the screen.

You okay? We took a quick coffee break, and I wanted to check in. Don't worry about the show, sweetheart. You'll always be a star in my book.

Reality raised its ugly hand of truth and smacked me in the face. What was the matter with me? How could I even think about leaving Keanu?

CHAPTER SEVENTEEN

Distraction was my middle name for the rest of the day. Like a robot, I waited on customers, turned in my orders, then promptly forgot what table went with which order. Poncho hollered at me twice, Vivian grew impatient, and much to my chagrin, Keanu's parents were back and huddled upstairs in the office, conducting business during his absence. To my relief, Terry left for the same meeting as Keanu at about three o'clock. On his way past, he'd grunted a "hello" but wouldn't meet my gaze.

I was too preoccupied with Howie's offer to worry about Terry right now. It still seemed unreal. This type of thing didn't happen to country girls like me. *I have an opportunity to go to Hollywood!* Millions of girls dreamed of this chance, but it belonged to me. *Me.* Ever since the tender age of nine, I'd been picking up my little pink desk lamp and giving Oscar acceptance speeches with it. Now I was being slated to act in a movie called—of all things—*Princes Can Be Charming.* How ironic.

The sad part was that I had already found my Prince Charming.

I'd texted Keanu back and explained that I hadn't been fired from the show—it was all a huge mistake, and I'd give him the details in person later. I also said that new information about Randolph and his college chums had surfaced and I'd like to get his input. He'd said he would pick up Chinese food and meet me at my apartment as soon as the meeting finished.

"What's with you?" Vivian asked after I'd delivered some food to an elderly couple out on the patio. "Something's bugging you."

"It's nothing. I'm a little stressed with everything going

on." I was fond of Viv, but like Tad, she had a hard time keeping things to herself. Unfortunately, Tad had refused to budge from the parking lot until I had told him what had happened. He swore that he wouldn't tell anyone, but this had to be eating away at him. Tad had as difficult of a time keeping a secret as I did trying *not* to snoop.

Vivian watched with interest as a pretty woman with sandy blonde hair entered the café from the lobby entrance. She was slightly taller than me and a few years older. She caught me staring and waved shyly in return. I recognized her as one of the surfing instructors who worked with my ex, Brad. I had broken off our relationship a few months back after discovering he'd been cheating on me. Since then I'd seen Brad on a few occasions but only from a distance. Each time he'd been with a different but equally gorgeous-looking girl.

In a strange way, I was grateful to my ex. If I hadn't followed him to Hawaii, I never would have met Keanu. As far as I was concerned, the two men were at complete opposites of the male spectrum.

Vivian gripped my arm in a sudden panic. "That's Samantha, who's dating Casey! And she's sitting in *my* section!"

Casey was an English bartender at The Lava Pot who'd had Vivian drooling all over herself for months. She'd done everything she could to get his attention, with the exception of running into The Lava Pot naked. From the rumors I'd heard circulating, it appeared Casey and Samantha were pretty tight. I didn't want to be mean but thought it might be time for Vivian to let go of her obsession.

Vivian's nails dug into my flesh, and I let out a small yelp of pain. "Down, girl. If it makes you feel any better, I'll wait on her."

She sighed despondently. "Please. I've heard she's nice, so that will only make things worse. I really need to go home and drown my sorrows in a glass of chardonnay."

Samantha glanced down at the menu and then looked over at us expectantly. I patted Vivian on the arm and approached the table. The young woman smiled up at me.

"Hi, Carrie, how are you?"

"Just fine. It's nice to see you, Samantha."

"Call me Sam." She ran a finger down the side of the laminated menu. "I'll have the pulled pork wrap with lettuce and tomato and an iced tea, please. I hate to be a pest, but is there any way to hurry up my order? I've got to get back and relieve Brad. He needs to take off early and doesn't like to be kept waiting."

"Sure, no problem." I took the menu from her outstretched hand. "Sounds like not much has changed with dear old impatient Brad. How's he doing these days?"

She rolled her eyes. "The same as ever. Don't get me wrong. He's one of the best surfers I've ever seen and really knows the sport. But that ego of his is bigger than the ocean."

"It is always growing, isn't it?" I mused. "Kind of like Poncho's homemade bread in the oven."

Samantha sighed. "He has a waiting list for students. Wish I did."

"Let me guess. All female?" I asked.

She gave me a wry grin. "You know it. I guess some women will never learn."

We had a good laugh together, and then I went to turn her order in to Poncho. Seeing his laptop on the nearby counter reminded me that I wanted to check on Wendy's status. "Is it okay if I borrow your computer for a second?" He was OCD about most things in the kitchen, but the laptop wouldn't be an issue for him.

"Help yourself." Poncho waved the order slip at me. "Is this for the surfer girl out there? She gives lessons to children, right?"

"She does." Brad couldn't stand kids, another one of his endearing qualities.

"When her order is ready, I will bring it out personally. I want to ask her about lessons for my boys."

Poncho was making Samantha's sandwich with one hand and using an electric mixer with the other. I watched as he dropped white chocolate chips, macadamia nuts, fresh pineapple, and coconut into the mixture.

"Is that cookie batter? It smells amazing."

Poncho cocked his head with pride. "These are my Aloha cookies. The dough must chill in the fridge for a bit, but they should be ready for you to sample before you leave."

"Can't wait."

Poncho's eyes observed me thoughtfully as I maneuvered the mouse. "What is wrong with you today? You have been very distracted and not as sharp as usual. And do not say 'nothing'—you cannot fool me."

It was the opportunity I'd been looking for. I needed to talk to somebody before I cracked. Besides Keanu, Poncho was the one person around here who could keep a secret, and I decided to take the plunge. "I've been offered a chance to go to Hollywood and screen test for a role in a movie. The director says there's a good chance I'll get the part."

Poncho's eyes widened. "That is incredible, *ho'aloha*!" The light suddenly faded from his face, and his expression grew somber. "But you would be leaving the Loco Moco. Do you think you would come back someday?"

I answered without hesitation. "Of course. Howie said I'd only be out there for a few months."

Poncho's mouth twitched into a grin underneath his slim moustache. "I am pretty sure your job here would be safe. You seem to have an *in* with the manager. What does Keanu say about all this?"

My mouth went dry. "I haven't told him yet."

He deftly raised one eyebrow. "Why not?"

"Because I only found out this afternoon and want to tell him in person. He's meeting me at my apartment tonight." My voice quivered like a little girl's. "Poncho, I'm not sure that I should go."

"This is what you have always wanted. Why would you not go?" He paused for a moment. "Ah. Because of Keanu. How serious are things between you two?"

I wasn't sure how comfortable I felt talking to Poncho about my love life. "He…he told me that he loved me."

Poncho placed the cookie dough in the fridge. "That does not surprise me. And do you love him?"

"Yes," I whispered. "But for some weird reason, I have a difficult time saying the actual words out loud. What's wrong with me?"

He went to the sink to wash his hands. "Nothing's wrong with you. There is a simple explanation. You are afraid of being hurt again, *ho'aloha*. All you have ever known is people who have broken your heart."

Poncho knew about my childhood. He'd experienced a rough life himself—a checkered past that included the accidental killing of another man. If there was anyone who understood about missed opportunities and the concept that life was too short to waste, it was him.

"You're right," I said honestly. "But I'm afraid I might lose him."

He patted my shoulder. "You have been through a lot, but do not shut Keanu out in the process. Do not be afraid to love him back. He is a good man, and I know how much he cares for you. He will not break your heart like that Cad did before."

"Brad," I joked. "His name was Brad."

He chuckled. "Do you not know about a play on words?"

Emotions overwhelmed me as I reached out to him. Although Poncho wasn't a demonstrative man, he allowed me to hug him, then patted my back awkwardly.

"Go to Keanu, little girl. Tell him what has happened. If you both truly care for each other, things will work themselves out."

I glanced at my watch. Six o'clock. Keanu had hoped that the meeting would be out by five thirty. If that was the case, he might already be at my apartment. "Okay, let me just finish this search first." I typed Wendy Ritzer's name into Google, and to my joy and surprise, a phone number with an 808 area code popped up. There was a picture of the woman and next to it read, *Your Happy Insurance Agent, on call 24 hours a day.*

I jotted her name and phone number down on a piece of paper then went into the back room to call her. Poncho was on the phone with his wife, and I felt certain he wouldn't hear me. The call was answered on its second ring.

"Wendy Ritzer." Her tone was brisk and businesslike.

"Hi, Miss Ritzer. I'm interested in some quotes for automobile insurance."

"Make, model, and year of the car, please."

Jeez, nice to meet you too. Since I didn't have a car, I used Keanu's for this purpose. "A 2017 Jeep Wrangler."

"Give me a phone number to reach you at, and I'll get

back to you shortly with a quote."

"Um," I hedged. "Could we possibly meet in person?"

"I don't usually do in-person meetings unless you're looking for life insurance, and they're no longer required for that either. Everything can be done over the phone, except for your medical exam."

"Oh! I forgot to mention that I did want life insurance as well. And I have lots of questions, so it would be great if we could meet."

She was silent for a moment, and I could hear the distinct rustle of papers on the other end. "Okay, I have some free time tomorrow afternoon."

"But I have to work at eleven," I protested. "Is there any chance we could meet at ten?"

The prolonged quiet spoke volumes, and I imagined Wendy cursing me out on the other end. "Fine. Where do you live? I'm in Kauai for the next couple of days."

I didn't want her coming to my house. "I work at the Aloha Lagoon Resort. Could we meet on the patio of The Lava Pot, say at ten o'clock?"

"I know the place," she said curtly. "What'd you say your name was?"

"Coral. Coral Palu." Sure, it was rotten to borrow Coral's name for this purpose but also kind of necessary.

"See you then." Wendy clicked off. Her abrupt manner warned me that she wouldn't be all that friendly, and it might be difficult to obtain any information. Maybe she weighed all her potential clients by the philosophy "Time is money."

Keanu had offered to come and pick me up, but I told him I'd meet him at the apartment. It was only a ten-minute walk, and I needed some air, plus time to think. There was still plenty of light left in the sky, and I was determined to clear the cobwebs from my brain.

When I went into the employee's room to gather my items I was surprised to see Ava standing there. She was placing some clean aprons inside the cubbies located above the lockers.

"Hello, Carrie." She smiled pleasantly.

"Hi, Ava." I reached for my purse and started to walk past her. "Have a great night."

She held up a hand. "Carrie, I was wondering if you had a minute to talk."

Oh boy. I tried not to think the worst but wondered if she might have heard Poncho and me chatting. That would prove to be a major embarrassment. Still, what choice did I have? The woman was my boss. "Sure, no problem."

She flushed slightly. "I wanted to apologize for everything that's happened. I know you never took that money. Terry knows it as well."

So why doesn't Terry tell me himself? "Ava, you have nothing to apologize for. You've been very good to me."

The blue eyes, so much like Keanu's, met mine and then shifted to the floor. "It's been hard on Terry. He's a changed man since we lost Kara." Her voice held a sudden catch. "I'm sure Keanu's told you about his sister."

A lump gathered in my throat. "Yes, he has. I wish I had words to express how sorry I am."

She bit into her lower lip. "Thank you. Losing Kara has made Keanu even more precious to us. It's a parent's worst nightmare to lose a child."

I was sure she was right. If my mother had ever lost Penny, she would have been devastated.

Ava seemed to guess my thoughts. "Keanu told me that you and your mother don't have much of a relationship and that you're virtually on your own. I'm truly sorry about that. It must be difficult."

As much as I liked Ava, I didn't want her pity. "Thanks, but I'm fine. Your son has been wonderful to me."

She smiled. "Keanu thinks the world of you, I can tell." She hesitated, groping for words. "I'd like for us to be friends, so if you ever need anything, please let me know."

I was touched by her concern. Keanu was lucky to have a mother like Ava. She was warm, friendly, and I'd never seen her raise her voice to anyone in the café. Ava was the complete opposite of her husband, but I did understand that grief affected people differently. Keanu himself had mentioned his father hadn't always been like that, so who was I to judge the man? There was no way to know what pain another person had endured, so I decided it was best to never make assumptions.

"Thank you," I said. "I'd like us to be friends too and know that it would make Keanu happy as well."

She sighed. "I hate to put so much on him, but Terry and I need to fly out to Arizona again as soon as possible. There are issues at some of our grocery stores. But we don't want to leave until we know what will happen with Randolph's wife—Miss Davenport."

I attempted to hold back a grimace. "I heard she was planning to sue."

Ava pinched the bridge of her nose between her thumb and forefinger. "Apparently she already has. We learned today that Miss Davenport filed a wrongful death suit with her attorney. The toxicology reports aren't back yet, but cyanide found in coffee prepared by the Loco Moco doesn't exactly make us look good."

Randolph hadn't been a saint, especially when you considered the way he'd treated Coral and her mother all these years. He'd also acted like everyone was beneath him. However, this so-called wife of his might be just as bad, or even worse. There were rumors of infidelity, a failed modeling career, and she was hungry for some cold, hard cash. Add these factors together, and I got killer. It should be obvious that Belinda was the one since she had the most to lose. So why was I convinced that there was still something missing from this equation?

"That's terrible," I said. "They're implicating me as well since I delivered the food."

She wrung her hands together in obvious frustration. "I wish Terry had never asked you to go."

"I didn't mean to suggest it was your fault in any way."

Ava gave me a warm, genuine smile. "I appreciate that. I really would like to get to know you better and want Keanu to bring you over for dinner some night when your show isn't on. We'd be honored to come to a performance as well."

Her words managed to tie my stomach in knots. The thought of Terry and Ava in the audience at *Little Women* was almost as nerve wracking as me on my own in Hollywood. *Shoot me now, please.* "That would be nice," I lied.

Ava patted my hand. "Well, you seem to be in a hurry, so tell my son I said hello." She winked and then started to climb the stairs back to the office.

I let myself out the patio entrance and started the walk toward my apartment. We'd had some rain earlier, but the day had turned glorious. The lush greenery around the island never ceased to amaze me. Brilliant sunlight reflected off the ocean and made the water appear even bluer than usual, while the tide had started to rush in. I longed to sit and daydream on the beach for a while, but real life was imminent.

Questions thundered through my head at a nonstop furious pace. *Should I stay, or should I go? How would I tell Keanu? Was there any chance that he could come with me?* Perhaps Detective Ray wouldn't allow me to leave the island until the murder had been solved. *Who was the person that had taken Randolph Cremshaw's life, and why did I feel that the disappearance of Sean Tyler over twenty years ago had something to do with it?*

I ran up the steps of my apartment and inserted my key into the door. Keanu was sitting on the couch, watching television. As always, he'd thrown his tie and jacket on the end table, and his white oxford shirt was rolled up at the elbows. He had a beer in one hand, and the other rubbed the top of Benny's head, who was curled contentedly in his lap. My heart warmed at the sight of them together, and I longed to come home to this visual every night.

"Hi, baby." Keanu rose to his feet and gently laid Benny on the couch. He walked over and planted a soft kiss on my lips then started toward the kitchen. "Ready to eat? I'm starved."

I stood there and watched as he removed silverware from a drawer and placed it on the small wooden table. He whistled softly as he set the plates on the table, as comfortable in the apartment as if it were his own. "So why did Jeff want to see you?" he asked suddenly.

Poncho's words from earlier flashed through my head, and something primal ignited inside me. I continued to follow Keanu's movements without speaking. In the few months that I had known this man, he had never once let me down or given me a reason to think he ever would. I worried about giving my heart away to him, but the truth was that it had happened months ago.

"Carrie?"

Keanu straightened up from the table and watched me with those beautiful eyes that were so easy to lose myself in. His expression was puzzled. "You okay?"

The thought of leaving him was so overwhelming that I couldn't bear it. For once in my life I had the two things I'd always been denied; a chance at a career I loved, and to be loved. Even though the relocation to Hollywood wouldn't be permanent, it still felt like I was being forced to decide between two things I wanted desperately. Life was so unfair at times.

Tonight, there would be no choices. I would have what I wanted.

"What's wrong?"

Keanu was standing very close to me, and the pupils of his eyes had darkened as he watched me. Without another word, I placed my arms around his neck and attacked his mouth in a greedy manner. He pulled me close against him and responded ardently. Within seconds our embrace became hotter than an inferno. Keanu tore his mouth away from mine and studied me, expression serious.

"Are you sure?" he asked softly as my heart continued to thunder away in my chest, so loud that I was positive he could hear.

My answer came promptly and without hesitation this time. "Yes. I'm sure that I love you."

CHAPTER EIGHTEEN

A sudden pressure awakened me. I opened one eye to see Benny staring down at me from his perch on my chest, an ominous scowl upon his face. He had positioned himself at such an angle that it was impossible for me to draw a deep breath. This was not unusual behavior for my furry feline. Any time I tried to sleep in and Benny's breakfast was late, it resulted in a similar occurrence.

After raising myself into a sitting position, I hugged the cat tightly to my chest. The smell of coffee infiltrated my nostrils as I leaned back against the headboard, and the curtains flapped around the open window behind me. A seabird outside of my window uttered a high-pitched whistle.

Sighing in content, I glanced at my watch. It was still twelve o'clock. *Aargh.* I'd have to get a new battery later today. This was driving me crazy.

I heard Keanu moving around in the kitchen, humming to himself. Heat burned my cheeks as I recalled the events from last night. Maybe it was the actress in me, but sometimes I couldn't help comparing movies to real life. My entire body tingled as I remembered feeling a bit like Scarlet O'Hara must have when Rhett Butler carried her up the stairs during *Gone with the Wind.* Unlike Scarlet though, I hadn't exactly been fighting Keanu off.

I was relieved that I hadn't mentioned the trip to California to him. It was pointless now anyway because I'd already decided not to go. Someday I'd have another chance. *Maybe.*

As I looked on my nightstand and tried to remember where I'd left my phone, Keanu's muscular form filled the doorway. For a few seconds he stood there, watching me in silence with a smile on his face that lit up the entire room. He held a cup of coffee in his hands and sat down on the edge of the bed, planting a soft kiss on my lips. "Morning, beautiful."

I stroked the unshaved stubble on his chin. "Good morning yourself."

His blue eyes shone with unrestrained happiness as he handed me the steaming mug. "Did you sleep well?"

I took a sip from the cup and then placed it on the nightstand. "Like a baby."

Keanu pulled me toward him, and we kissed again—this time, a long and lingering one that left me breathless. I tasted coffee and mint-flavored toothpaste and savored the smell of his cologne—a woodsy musk scent. Like the rest of him, it was intoxicating.

After we broke apart, he cradled my face gently between his hands. "Thank you for last night. I'll treasure it always."

My entire body tingled at the words. "Me too."

His voice was low and sexy. "I'd love an encore right now, but unfortunately I've got to rush home and put on a monkey suit. Then I need to get over to the café to pay some bills and be at the resort for an eleven o'clock meeting. Thank God this is the last one, and then everyone will be flying back to Arizona tonight, so things can finally get back to normal around here."

"What time is it?" I asked.

He nuzzled my hair. "Eight thirty. You're working at eleven, right?"

I ran my hands over his bare rock-hard chest. "Eleven to six. How about dinner around seven? I'll make us something here."

Keanu straightened up and made a face. "I might be kind of late. Since it's the last day of meetings, you never know how long these things tend to get drawn out. All the stores are having issues, from back stabbing between the employees to not enough profits, and we've been trying to figure out some new schematics. Dad even wants to clean house at one of the stores. Who knows how long this might take."

"That's all right. I'm not going anywhere, so whenever

you get here is fine." I glanced around the room. "Have you seen my phone?"

He rose from the bed. "Yeah, you left it on the coffee table last night. I'll grab it."

"Thanks." I watched him leave the bedroom and sipped my coffee like a lady of leisure. When we had first started dating, I'd promised myself that I wasn't going to rush into another relationship. I'd been wary of men after my tumultuous experience with Brad and wanted to take things slow. Keanu understood and had never pushed me. The bond between us had been strong from the beginning, and now it was unbreakable. Despite my initial vigilance, I'd fallen—and fallen hard for him.

I took another long sip from the mug and decided to call Howie after Keanu left, to thank him for the opportunity but also tell him that I had decided not to go to California after all. Howie would probably try to talk me out of it, and Jeff might too, but it was no use. My mind was made up.

Keanu came back into the bedroom as I continued to stroke Benny's fur. He'd been staring down at the screen of my phone and now glanced up at me with a puzzled expression. Benny jumped off the bed, as if he had a sudden premonition. The rigid stance of Keanu's body told me that something was very wrong.

"What is it?" Suddenly I feared the worst.

He said nothing as he handed the phone to me. There was a text from Tad that had literally come in seconds ago. The phone might have even lit up with the incoming message while Keanu had brought it to me. Of all the worse luck. It read: *Good morning, Miss Hollywood! Have you told K the news yet? When will you be leaving for California? I want to throw a super bash before you go. A Khardashian-sized blast. Love ya, toots.*

Okay, forget about looking for a killer. I might turn into one the next time I saw Tad.

I bit into my lower lip and forced myself to meet Keanu's piercing gaze. He stood there with his arms folded across his chest as he waited for me to say something. I knew he was upset and couldn't fault him for that.

"Why didn't you tell me?" Keanu's voice was low, but it was obvious from his expression that he was upset. I actually would have preferred yelling and screaming over the pained look in his eyes.

A dull ache formed in the middle of my chest. The last thing I ever wanted to do was hurt him. Sheepishly, I stared down at the blankets.

"Carrie?"

"I don't know," I whispered to the fuzzy yellow comforter. "I just wanted to be with you last night and not think about anything else."

Keanu sat down on the edge of the bed and placed a finger under my chin. "Look at me."

I gazed into his deep-set eyes and fought to hold back a sob. Didn't he understand *why* I hadn't told him? Keanu loved me—he was the only person who ever had. I couldn't throw that away now. My throat grew tight with tears. "It doesn't matter because I've already made my decision. I'm not going."

Keanu's jaw dropped. "Care, that's insane. You *have* to go."

I must have heard him wrong. How could he tell me that after the night we had just shared? "No, I'm not leaving you."

His shoulders sagged. "I don't want that either. The thought of you going depresses the hell out of me. But if you stayed here—because of me—well, do you really think that's going to make either one of us happy?"

"What do you mean?"

Keanu wove his fingers through my hair. "You'd be turning down the chance of a lifetime. This is your dream. You might grow to resent me after a while."

I shook my head furiously. "That would never happen."

He sighed. "You say that now, but who knows? How long would you be gone for?"

"Howie said three months at the most. But there's a good chance they won't even want me, and I'd be back within a week." My voice sounded too hopeful.

Keanu wrinkled his forehead. "If I was a betting man, I'd say that won't happen. In fact, I'd stake my life on the notion that the role is already yours. I couldn't be prouder of you, baby."

Tears dripped down my cheeks and onto the comforter. Keanu wiped them away and then brushed his lips across mine.

"No more crying, okay? I don't want the lady I love to ever be sad."

"I love you too." There was a growing need inside of me to keep repeating the words to him, a sudden urgency that had transpired since last night. I'd been starved for affection for what seemed like an eternity. Now that I'd finally been fed, my hunger refused to subside.

He ran a finger across my lips. "I'm a lucky guy."

"It's taken me a while to say those three words to you, even though I felt them right from the beginning. No one ever told me before that they—" The waterworks started again. *When had I turned into such a cry baby?*

He reached out and enveloped me in his strong arms. "I know, Carrie. I figured it might be something like that." Keanu kissed my hair softly. "Go ahead and cry, sweetheart. Let it all out."

That was it—I was officially a goner now. Keanu stroked my hair while I sobbed into his arms. Last night had been special, the most wonderful night of my life. But now it would be even more difficult to leave him. What on earth had I been thinking?

He released his hold on me and cradled my face between his hands. "Listen. I told you before that I'm not going anywhere. I'll be right here waiting when you get back from California. Maybe I can even swing a couple of visits out there too."

My heart gave a sudden leap. "Really? That would be fantastic. Do you think you'd be headed out that way anytime soon?"

Keanu's body tensed against mine. "My father wants me to leave the Loco Moco and take over the CEO position in Arizona. He's planning on firing the current head suit out there."

My heart gave another leap—right into the pit of my stomach. Now it was my turn to be the accusatory. "How long have you known?"

"A couple of days," he replied. "I was going to tell you last night—before we got involved with other matters." He flashed his dimple at me. "Carrie, it doesn't matter, because I told him yesterday that I'm not going."

"That must have gone over well," I said dryly. "I'll bet

my name got mentioned too." No doubt Terry would think I'd put his son up to the decision.

He kissed me again. "Yes, he did bring up your name, and that made me furious. I told him not to drag you into this because you were not to blame. If they need me to fly out there occasionally to help, fine. But Kauai is my home, and I'm happy at the Loco Moco. I don't want to leave here. And when you come back," he added smoothly, "maybe we can talk about making some more permanent living arrangements. You, me, and Ben under one roof. How does that sound?"

"Yes," I whispered. "I'd love that." To be able to wake up next to him every morning would be another dream come true.

As if on cue, Benny jumped back on the bed. He meowed at Keanu, as if giving his approval of the plan too. Keanu laughed and stretched out a hand to scratch him behind his ears. "I wish I could take him while you're gone. Let me talk to my landlord."

"It's okay," I reassured him. "When Tad found out about the screen test yesterday, he practically begged me to let him move in here. His uncle is redoing the apartment building, and Tad needs a place to crash for a few months. He's supposed to stop over at some point today and take measurements for a chair he wants to bring along. That reminds me. Can you leave your key under the mat for him?"

"Sure, but why doesn't he just move in with his parents? They live local, and he could save some money that way," Keanu said.

I shook my head. "Tad would rather die than move back in with his parents. If the renovations are done before I get back from California, he said he'll bring Benny back to his place. Then I'll take over paying Arnie rent again." Arnie was my landlord, and I already knew he wouldn't have a problem with Tad staying here. "If...if I decide to go, that is."

Keanu's ocean blue eyes rested on me solemnly. "I thought it was already decided."

I knew what I was about to suggest was impossible, but I went ahead and asked it anyway. "Is there any chance that you could go with me?"

Keanu was quiet for a moment as he processed my question. "I want to, Carrie, more than anything. But when I refused to go to Arizona, I promised my father I'd stay here and run the Loco Moco single handedly since he and Mom expect to be out there quite a bit in the next few months. Let me talk to them again. Maybe we can work out some other solution."

"No." I didn't want to come between Keanu and his parents. "That was selfish of me to ask. I know you have responsibilities here you can't ignore. It's just going to be so hard—without you there."

He kissed me lightly on the lips. "You'll be so busy putting in twelve-hour-day shoots that you won't even miss me."

"That's not true." Keanu consumed my thoughts constantly. He'd become my opium, and I didn't know how I'd function without him, especially after last night.

"I hate the idea of you being out there all by yourself," Keanu admitted. "This director, the guy I met at the Hana Hou—Howie, right? Are you sure he isn't some type of letch? The kind that preys on young girls and gives them parts so they'll sleep with him?"

I jumped out of bed and grabbed my robe that was flung at the bottom. "I don't think Howie's like that." The conversation I'd overheard at Hana Hou yesterday replayed itself inside my head. Did Howie have something to do with Randolph's murder? And what did he and Jeff really know about the disappearance of Wendy's boyfriend, Sean?

"I didn't get a chance to tell you, but it turns out that the same night as Jeff's college play, a student from the campus disappeared. His name was Sean Tyler and he was never heard from again. He also happened to be dating the female lead of the show. It seemed like a weird coincidence to me."

Keanu took my hand and started to lead me toward the living room. "We'll have to put our heads together tonight and see what we can come up with. I'm already late, but I have a surprise for you before I leave. Come on—it's in here." He pointed at the end table, where a beautiful display of red roses sat in a crystal vase.

My mouth dropped open in amazement. "Where did these come from? There's no flower shops open at this hour."

He grinned. "One of the local florists is a good friend of mine. I arranged it with him last night after you fell asleep. He delivered the vase personally a little while ago. Do you like them?"

I leaned down to inhale their fragrant scent. Seriously, what was there not to like, or love, about this man? "They're beautiful. You're so good to me."

He placed his arms around my waist. "It's about time someone was."

As I hugged him back, I spotted the piece of paper on the coffee table with Wendy's number. "By the way, I'm meeting Wendy Ritzer at ten o'clock under the pretense that I need car insurance. She was the lead in Jeff's college show and dated Sean Tyler. I want to see if she'll talk to me."

Keanu drew his eyebrows together. "You're a complete stranger. What makes you think she'll tell you anything?"

"Don't worry. I have a plan."

He gave me a doubtful look. "I'll bet. Where are you meeting her? In a public place? I can leave work for a while if you need me to be there."

"I should be fine alone. I'll be right outside The Lava Pot, and you know that people are always around. There's nothing to worry about."

"Maybe you should call Detective Ray and tell him about your hunch," he said.

"But I can't prove anything yet." I pointed at the crates that sat underneath my glass-topped coffee table. "We have to get these back to Coral soon. I've looked through all the other papers but didn't find anything useful."

He nudged one of the crates with the toe of his sneaker. "Okay. Tomorrow or the next day I'll drop them off to her." He gave me a swift kiss. "You look tired. I guess that's my fault, huh?" He grinned like a naughty little boy.

I smiled. "Yes, but you're forgiven."

Keanu pushed the hair back from my face. "If it's slow and you need to take off early from work to start *my* dinner, feel free."

"My boss gives me preferential treatment," I teased.

"Well, just don't tell anyone." He grabbed his car keys

from the table. "Only one more of these blasted meetings and then things can get back to normal. I'll be at the café for a little while but will probably be gone before you get there. Text me after you meet this woman so I know everything is okay. What do you want to do after dinner tonight? Go clubbing or take in a movie?"

"Staying in with you sounds wonderful," I said honestly.

A sly smile spread across his face. "I'm sure I can come up with *something* that we can do here."

I laughed and leaned my head against his chest. "You're all that I need or want. Hollywood can wait."

Keanu held me close. "It's all going to work out fine, sweetheart. I promise you that."

CHAPTER NINETEEN

———

After Keanu left, I took a shower, ate a bowl of cereal, and had a second cup of coffee. It was past nine thirty then, so I gave Benny a hug and took off for Aloha Lagoon. The day had an eerie, foreboding characteristic to it, and the overcast sky seemed to share in that illusion. I'd grown used to the heat while living here, but today's humidity was overly oppressive, more than enough to leave one gasping for air.

The Lava Pot didn't open until eleven o'clock, which was fine with me. I didn't drink much—especially at this time of day—and now wouldn't have to worry that Casey the bartender might see me and unintentionally blow my cover.

From this particular spot, there was a fabulous view of the white sand beach where a woman was busy instructing a group of kids with surf boards. The tables outside the bar were deserted, except for two. A man and a woman who appeared to be in their thirties sat talking quietly, holding hands with their Starbucks cups in front of them.

I spotted a woman at another table wearing white capri pants and a pink lace blouse. She was busy texting on her phone. A large day planner lay open on the table, and a black briefcase was on the chair beside her.

I veered in her direction and she immediately looked up. "Miss Ritzer?"

Wendy put the phone down and rose to her feet, extending a well-manicured hand. "Coral? Nice to meet you. Have a seat."

She shuffled some papers while I took a moment to study her. Wendy was heavyset, with titian-colored hair worn in a short bob and a dusting of freckles across her tiny nose.

Profound wrinkles surrounded her brown eyes and creased her forehead. I knew that she was in her early forties, but the crow's feet gave the impression of someone much older.

"Okay," Wendy said. "Since you're so young, the whole life insurance policy is the best way for you to go. It's also the best value. I've brought some pamphlets—"

Time to put my acting skills to work. "Miss Ritzer, you went to college with Randolph Cremshaw, didn't you?"

Her mouth fell open, and for a moment it seemed that she didn't comprehend what I had said. "What does that have to do with your insurance?"

"You know that he died the other day, right?"

In a sudden fury, she slammed the planner shut. "Look. I don't know who you are or what you're getting at but—" Realization dawned, and she shook her head in disbelief. "Oh, I get it. You're not interested in buying anything from me. This is some kind of setup." She started to rise from the table.

I touched her arm. "Please wait. It's not what you think. Randolph was my father."

I prayed that my facial expressions wouldn't fail me now. From the look she shot me, it appeared that I had succeeded.

"Oh my," she breathed. "I'm sorry for your loss but haven't seen your father in years."

"I'm looking into his death and need your help."

She picked up a tissue and wiped at the sweat that had started to gather on her forehead. "Why me? What can I do? Like I said, it's been years since I've seen him."

"I've been going through his old papers," I said, "and thought you two might have had some type of relationship."

She eyed me suspiciously. "We were in English literature class and did some dopey play together. That was all. I didn't sleep with him." Wendy paused for a moment. "At least I don't think so."

Wow. "I wondered if his death might tie in somehow with your boyfriend's disappearance back then."

Her head whipped around toward me in surprise. "Sean? That was over twenty years ago. There is *no* connection. You're grasping at straws here. Anyhow, the police are checking into

Randy's death, right? Why don't you leave this to them?"

"I don't trust them," I lied. "I loved my father and want to know the truth, so I'm launching my own investigation. I found out that your boyfriend disappeared the same night as the show you were in, *Destiny in December*."

Wendy tapped her pen on the table. "That's right. To tell you the truth, I don't remember much about that night. I had way too much to drink. I was still in a fog when I talked to the cops the next day. I told them I didn't know anything, and that part still hasn't changed."

"There was a cast party after the show, wasn't there?" I prompted her. "Dad kept a journal and mentioned it." I was amazed at how freely the lies were flowing out of my mouth again. "Was your boyfriend there too?"

She laughed. "Some boyfriend. Sean got pissed whenever he saw me talking to another guy. He wasn't very likeable, shall we say. I'm not surprised that he disappeared."

I wondered what she meant. "Do you remember seeing him at the theater that evening? Maybe he happened to see you, um, talking with another guy?"

She chuckled. "Honey, I was three sheets to the wind that night. I could have slept with Brad Pitt and not remembered. Yeah, your father was right. We did have a cast party after the show backstage. No food, but plenty of drinks. We all got trashed."

She paused for a sip from her water bottle, and I waited patiently for her to continue.

"Everyone else had left except for me and this one guy. We ah—started to get cozy, if you get my drift."

Yikes. I so did not want to hear this.

She gave an embarrassed little laugh. "I must have blacked out after all the booze because I don't remember anything else. The next thing I knew it was daylight, and I was lying outside, next to the dumpster by the back door. At least I had clothes on. I got up, dusted myself off, and went back to my dorm. What a mother of a headache I had all day."

This didn't make any sense. "Could Sean have been there? Do you think he and the guy you were with had a fight?'"

"It's possible," she admitted. "Like I said though, it's

been over 20 years. How could Sean's disappearance back then have anything to do with Randy's death the other day?"

Detective Ray would have been proud of my line of questioning. Maybe. "Do you think that Sean is still alive?"

Wendy's face clouded over, and she hesitated for a moment before she answered. "No, I don't. Look. I'm sorry about your father, but I'm done talking about this. It's a part of my life I'd prefer not to rehash."

"Understood," I said quickly, afraid that she might try to bolt. "Perhaps Sean saw you and the other guy—um, involved? Maybe he tried to beat him up. Who were you with?"

Wendy's voice became a low, angry growl. "I told you— I don't remember who it was. After a while all those college guys start to look alike."

Gross. How many guys had this woman actually slept with back then? Forget it. I didn't want to know. "Do you think your partner that night could have killed Sean?"

"No idea," she hissed. "The semester ended the following week, and I never went back to school."

"Why not?" I wondered if she might have gotten pregnant.

"If you must know, my mom was sick, so I had to stay home and take care of her. Family obligations. You know what that's like."

Actually, I didn't but said nothing.

"Hey, Carrie, how's it going?"

Startled, I almost jumped out of my seat. Casey was standing beside our table, the warm wind blowing through his curly, light brown blondish hair. "Can I get you ladies a drink? I'm about to open up."

Wendy looked puzzled. "I thought you said your name was Coral."

"It is." I gave Casey my best death glare. "You must have me confused with someone else, mister."

He held up both hands in amusement and spoke in that charming English accent of his. "No worries. We're cool."

Wendy tossed the rest of her papers in her briefcase. "I don't know what kind of game you're trying to pull with me, honey, but I've had about enough. Don't call me again."

"Wendy, it's not what you—"

Before I could say another word, she picked up her briefcase and hurried away without even a backward glance at me.

I continued to sit there lost in thought for a few minutes. Casey watched me intently from a nearby table as he wiped it down but made no attempt to come near me again. I knew I should explain what had happened but wasn't feeling very sociable right now. I started to dial Detective Ray's number and then stopped myself. What on earth would I say? This was all speculation on my part, but I had a disturbing feeling that Sean had come looking for Wendy that night and found her in a delicate position with another man. What if Wendy had killed Sean herself? Or perhaps she was covering for someone. But who?

I reached into my purse for the playbill I'd brought along and studied it for the umpteenth time. Jeff, Richard, Randolph, and Howie. My stomach churned as I read the names. Could Howie or Jeff be a killer? What would their motive be? Richard or Belinda probably stood to inherit money. Could they have been acting together, like a team? Perhaps this didn't tie in with Sean's disappearance at all, but my intuition warned me that the date of the play back then was too much of a coincidence to overlook.

Maybe I could find out from Jeff where Richard lived. I would love to question him further. Or I could try to hang around at the Aloha Lagoon for another glimpse of him. My brain continued to sort out the list of virtual suspects. What about Coral? I doubted that she had been completely honest with Keanu and me. Would she inherit Randolph's wealth now, or did her mother have something to do with the crime? Jonathan from Starlight might figure into the equation as well. He loathed Randolph and had admitted that he'd pushed him in a fit of anger. What if Randolph had threatened again to go public and Jonathan longed to shut him up…permanently?

Absently I glanced down at the time on my phone. Five minutes to eleven. Shoot! I silently chastised myself for being late to work. I'd never done that before. Now I'd have to wait until this evening to get my watch fixed, unless it was slow enough at the café for me to take a break this afternoon. There was a small jewelry store located across from that cute dress boutique in the resort's courtyard. Hopefully they stayed open past six.

As I hurried toward the Loco Moco, an image of Detective Ray popped into my head. Although he wouldn't provide me with any further details, I was fairly certain Randolph's death had been caused by cyanide. I'd have to check Poncho's laptop to see where someone might be able to purchase the deadly powder. There had to be a certain risk factor involved with buying it online, unless the killer had obtained it in a different manner.

Tad was on his way out of the café with a bag of dirty linens over his shoulder when I rushed past him toward the back kitchen door.

He made a *tsk-tsk* sound and wagged his finger at me. "Gotta stop those late nights with the K-man."

I yelled over my shoulder at him. "Remind me to strangle you later for that text you sent."

"What gives? I thought Hollywood socialites loved parties!" he called out. "Come on—it'll be a blast. I'm going clubbing with some friends tonight. Text ya later, doll."

My response was an air wave as I zoomed into the kitchen and promptly barreled right into Vivian, who was carrying a plate of eggs and a cup of coffee. The dish flew into the air, somersaulted a few times, and then landed inches away from a very annoyed chef at the stove.

"Carrie!" Poncho shouted angrily. "You need to be more careful."

Breathing heavily, I stooped to my knees to pick up the mess, and Vivian joined me. "Girl, what has gotten into you lately?" she asked.

"Sorry, Viv. I'm a hot mess today."

"No kidding." She examined my face closely for a second while I picked up the cracked pieces of the dish.

"What?" I asked.

She grinned and whispered so low that Poncho couldn't hear. "I *know*. It's written all over your face. Congratulations.""

My cheeks were on fire. "Cripes, Viv! You are

unbelievable."

Vivian let out a small sigh as she grabbed a broom next to the sink. "Sorry. I'm living vicariously through your life. I have to admit that I'm a teensy bit jealous."

The expression on her face tugged at my heart strings. "You'll find a great guy soon. I know you will." How could she not? She was pretty, intelligent, and fun to be with. Didn't the local guys know what they were missing?

I threw the remnants of the meal into the trash, stood up, and glanced in the direction of the back room, which led to the stairs and office. "Did Keanu leave yet?"

Vivian grinned. "Over an hour ago. Come on, details, please."

I rolled my eyes. "Just stop, okay?"

Poncho grunted. "If you two are done with your love gossip session, Terry said that the storage closet could use a good cleaning. Sybil's waiting on a table, and since it is so slow, this would be a good time."

"Hey, Ponch." Vivian removed her apron and set it on the counter. "Care needs an ice cream cone. Mind if we take a fifteen-minute break?"

His mouth dropped open as he pointed at me. "She just got here!"

"Oh, have a heart," Vivian crooned. "We never take breaks, and the closet can wait. We'll bring you back some too. What kind do you want?"

He narrowed his eyes. "None. I know what you are up to. It is girl-talk time. Or more like, it is *Keanu* talk time." He waved the spatula at her. "Be back in 15 minutes."

Vivian giggled as she grabbed my hand and half dragged me toward the kitchen door. "You're swell, Ponch."

"Stop calling me that," he growled and turned back to the stove.

"Come on." Vivian shut the door behind her. "Let's run over to Island Delights for a cone. My treat."

"I could use a sugar fix right about now," I admitted.

She slung an arm around my shoulders as we walked toward the courtyard of the resort, where the ice cream shop was located right next to the Happy Hula Dress Shop. I thought about my watch repair again then dismissed it from my mind.

"You're so lucky," Vivian said. "Keanu's gorgeous and a sweetheart of a guy. It sounds like he really loves you. The men I've dated have only been interested in one thing, if you get my drift."

"You're right, I *am* lucky. I'm not used to a guy treating me well either, probably because of everything that happened with Brad. I really love him, Viv."

"I'm so happy for your both." She hesitated, her gaze fixed on me. "There's something I should tell you."

A twinge of doubt ran through me. "What? About Keanu?"

She shook her head as we went inside the shop and waited in line. Vivian looked around, and once she was convinced that no one was listening, she leaned closer. "Brad came into the café last week. You had just left. He was teasing me and talking about how pretty I was and then asked me to go out with him. When I told him I'd never do that to you, he said, oh, she doesn't have to know."

Sadly, this came as no surprise. "Yeah, that sounds about Brad's speed."

"He asked for ice water, so I brought a glass over and promptly dumped it in his lap." She grinned at the memory. "Good thing Terry wasn't around. I told Keanu about it afterward, and he seemed rather pleased."

I laughed out loud. "You're a good friend, Viv."

"Hey, I try." She studied the chalkboard behind the display case that had today's flavors written on it. "What are you having? I'm in the mood to try Guava Galore."

We gave our order to the young blond man behind the counter, who Vivian flirted shamelessly with as she paid for the cones. I ordered chocolate coconut, which hit the spot on a humid day like this. We grabbed napkins and looked around for a seat outside among the crowded tables.

Vivian grabbed my arm. "Holy cow. Look at the table to the far left. Is that who I think it is?"

Two slim women with long, shimmering black hair had their backs to us. One of them was spooning ice cream out of a cup while she chatted with the other woman. She dropped her napkin and bent to retrieve it. I saw the low-cut tight T-shirt and knew instantly who it was. When she straightened up, our eyes met.

Coral was almost an exact replica of her mother—the long sleek hair, soulful dark eyes, red lips, and high cheekbones. The woman had to be in her forties, but she could easily have passed for Coral's sister. It made me wonder what someone who looked like her had ever seen in rude, foot-fungal Randolph, but hey, to each his own. Maybe he'd been different back then—charming in some strange sort of way and had swept her off her feet like a gallant prince. I had my doubts though.

"Come on." I gave Vivian a nudge. "That must be Coral's mother, and I want to talk to her."

"Are you crazy? Keanu fired Coral. And she hates you, remember."

"We have sort of a truce now." I started walking toward the table, Coral's eyes still glued on me.

"Oh really?" Vivian looked amused. "When did this happen?"

"I'll tell you about it later. Just follow my lead."

Coral's cheeks flushed pink as we approached. "Hi."

"Hi, Coral."

Coral's mother looked up at both of us and smiled. "Hello. Are these friends of yours, Coral?"

"Uh." Coral's eyes searched mine intently, as if pleading for me to not say anything.

I extended my hand. "Hi, I'm Carrie, and this is Vivian. We work at the Loco Moco."

The woman patted the seat next to her. "I'm Sefina. Why don't you girls join us?"

Coral rolled her eyes, obviously wishing that we would disappear. Vivian didn't wait for a second invitation. She plopped herself down on Coral's bench, leaving me the empty seat next to Sefina.

Sefina's smile was warm and genuine. "It's lovely to meet you both. Coral told me that she was let go because the café was slow. Did that happen to you too?"

I knew that Coral wouldn't tell her mother the truth about why she'd been fired. Vivian had already been filled in by

Poncho, and her mouth dropped open when Sefina spoke. "Well no," she stammered. "Because—"

I shot Vivian a warning look. "Vivian and I haven't been fired yet. We've been there longer than Coral, so unfortunately it was a situation of last hired, first fired."

Sefina sighed. "Yes, I was afraid of something like that. I'm sorry that business is so bad."

Okay, if Coral was going to lie about her reason for being fired, then I was going to take this opportunity to grill her mother. Richard's words were still fresh in my head. "You do know why we're slow, right? It's been like that ever since Coral's father was killed."

Coral shot me a look that clearly said she intended to murder me when we were alone. Sefina, to my surprise, didn't even blink.

"I wasn't aware that Coral had told you who her father was." She twisted her napkin between her slim fingers and stared pointedly at her daughter. "She didn't have very kind feelings toward him, I'm afraid."

"The Loco Moco is under suspicion for his death because I served him coffee that had cyanide in it," I said.

Sefina set her ice cream cup down on the table and nodded. "I once loved him very much, and was sad and shocked to hear about his death. Unfortunately, he was not the man I thought he was. When he found out I was pregnant, he decided the fun times were over. He never wanted children." She shook her head. "Men. I don't know what they think sometimes."

Vivian snorted. "They do their thinking with a different part of the body than their brain."

"Not all of them," I said defensively, thinking again how fortunate I was. "Have you talked to the police about his death?"

"Oh sure. Coral and I have both been questioned. It seems that Randy's wife told the cops exactly where to find us. Some detective named Ray grilled us like a swordfish. He probably thinks we're responsible for Randy's death, but I don't care. The entire thing was *poho*."

I smiled, grateful that I knew what the word meant now.

Sefina laughed, but it sounded bitter. "What did they think, that I tracked the man down in his hotel room to get revenge on him for leaving me 20 years ago? Why bother after all this time?"

I noticed that Coral had started to squirm in her seat. Maybe she was afraid her mother might have bothered? Or perhaps Coral had done the deed herself to get revenge for Sefina. "When's the last time you saw him?"

Sefina looked at me in surprise. "I spoke with him on the phone a few weeks ago. I asked him to please reconsider helping Coral with her tuition, and of course he refused again. Why do you ask?"

"Oh, no reason," I said quickly. "I'm sorry the Loco Moco had to let Coral go. It's so difficult for college kids to find jobs these days."

"Very true," Sefina murmured.

"So, what do you do for a living?" What I really wanted to know was, *do you get Saturdays off in case you plan to kill someone?*

"I'm a dental assistant," she replied. "It took me a long time to finish my schooling, but I finally made it. I wish I could help Coral out with her tuition more. I'm so proud of her. She's determined to do it all on her own."

Uh-huh. With a little help from the Loco Moco too. "Do you work Monday through Friday?"

Coral's jaw locked in a defiant manner. She knew exactly where I was going with this line of questioning. "I think we'd better leave, Mom. I want to get to the bank before it closes."

Sefina glanced from me to her daughter. "Yes, I do work Monday through Friday, but the dentist who employs me was on vacation last week, so I did some spring cleaning around the house and other things. I go back to work tomorrow."

Coral jumped to her feet and threw her napkin and cup in the trash. "Time to leave, Mom."

Sefina rose to her feet and nodded at us. "Nice meeting you, girls. Hope to see you again."

"Likewise." Vivian narrowed her eyes at Coral. "Do take care."

Coral grabbed her mother's arm, and they walked away, leaving us to stare after them. Vivian came around to my side of the table, hands on her hips. "What gives? Do you think one of them did it?"

"I hope not, but they both did have motives." I'd have to check and see if I could find any more information on Sefina Palu later. Was she too sweet and nice for her own good? Or had she just given a performance to rival one at the Hana Hou?

CHAPTER TWENTY

───────

Shortly after Vivian and I returned to the Loco Moco, customers started to flock in, and I was glad to be so busy for a change. It gave me less time to think. The rest of the day flew by, and there were no opportunities for any further breaks or to even check my phone for messages until after four o'clock. I went into the kitchen for a glass of water when my phone vibrated in my pants pocket. I withdrew it eagerly, positive it must be a text from Keanu. No such luck.

Rehearsal tonight at 7 pm. Just actors and assistant director. See you then.

Jeff. My heart sank with disappointment. I had really wanted to make dinner for Keanu and have a quiet evening alone with him. I was tempted to send a message back and say I wasn't feeling well. Jeff always pulled this last-minute stuff, and it was growing tiresome. Yes, the show was important, but all of the actors had jobs and lives. What if I'd had to work this evening? Plus, I didn't even have a way to get there.

Keanu hadn't been positive what time his meeting would let out. If I walked to the theater, it would take me close to an hour, and I hated to spend money on a cab. Tad was busy, and Vivian had already left to go shopping with a friend. Poncho would be here until closing and planned to prepare some extra desserts.

I texted Jeff back. *I don't have a way to get there. Sorry.*

His reply came back almost immediately. *Just because you are going to Hollywood, do not think you can cop an attitude with me. I'll pick you up. Be ready at six thirty. Sharp.*

Jeff had given me rides home a few times before, so he knew where I lived. I fumed at his message in silence. *What attitude?* Did he really think I was going to become all pretentious and pompous now? If so, the man didn't know me at all. He'd also been the one who'd encouraged me to go to Hollywood. The urge to send back a nasty response was tempting, but I counted to ten first and then merely typed, *Okay. Thank you.*

Before I went back into the café, I typed out a message to Keanu. *Jeff just texted. We have another freakin' rehearsal tonight. So mad! I wanted to spend the evening with you. Can you pick me up from the theater about ten, and then we'll go back to my place? Love you.*

It wasn't until I was about to leave the café at six o'clock when I realized that Keanu had never texted me back. This meant the meeting was most likely going longer than anticipated. He probably hadn't even looked at his phone yet. Well, he'd see the text before he left for my apartment.

I called out a goodbye to Sybil and Poncho and departed through the back door of the kitchen. I glanced down at my watch then did a mental head slap and turned in the direction of the jewelry shop. Did I even have time to get the battery installed? I'd feed Benny when I got home and then grab a piece of fruit to munch on the way to the theater. Keeping Jeff waiting was not an option since he didn't know the meaning of patience these days.

I hurried down the boardwalk in the direction of the stores and didn't even glance in the direction of the Happy Hula Dress Shop. This was no time for distractions. As I rushed into Liko's Jewelry Store, I noticed the sign said that they were open until seven. Luck must have been on my side because the only person inside was an elderly Polynesian man behind the counter.

The man looked up as I rushed in. He must have been about eighty, his entire body shrunken from age. He had a tuft of white hair on the top of his head, and his leathery face and neck were lined with massive wrinkles that deepened further as he smiled at me.

"Can I help you, miss?" he asked.

I held out my watch. "This needs a new battery, please." If I was thrifty, I'd have taken it back to the jewelry store where I'd gotten the watch fixed last time, when I'd gone shopping with

Keanu on the island of Oahu. But there was no time for that now. "Are you the owner?"

He nodded proudly and patted his chest. "Liko is my name, and jewelry is my game." He squinted down at the watch and then placed it on the glass-topped counter. "I need to get a different tool. Be right back." He shuffled into the back room, his gait reminding me of Tim Conway from the comical old Carol Burnett reruns I used to love to watch as a child. What a cute old man.

I glanced at the tray of diamond rings inside the polished case and drew a deep breath. It was silly to even think about this now. We'd only been dating for a few months and neither one of us was ready for marriage. Still, a part of me longed for that security someday, along with the house and a little white picket fence. Maybe even—

A sudden crash from the next room jolted me out of my thoughts. Alarmed, I ran behind the counter and into the adjoining back area. Liko was flat on his back, attempting to raise himself into a sitting position.

"Are you all right?" I helped the man to his feet.

Liko looked slightly embarrassed as he nodded. "The eyesight isn't what it used to be, I'm afraid." He pointed at the step stool lying on its side. "I didn't even see the stool until I went flying over it." He smiled wryly and adjusted his glasses on his face.

I laughed, relieved that he was okay, and started to follow him out of the room. I gazed up idly at the steel shelving propped against the wall. There were several small bottles of jewelry cleaner and some unidentifiable boxes. A large white container stood out from the rest. The word *Cyanide* was printed on it in large black letters.

I continued to stare at the container, fascinated.

"Miss?" Liko was standing in the doorway, watching me with a puzzled expression.

"Sorry." Distracted, I walked back into the storefront and tried to process what I had just seen. Liko opened the watch while I struggled to pose my question in a nonchalant manner. "I was wondering why a jeweler would need cyanide."

Ugh. Way to be subtle, Care.

He stared up at me, a frown further deepening the lines in his forehead. "I keep forgetting to get rid of that. EPA regulations are tough these days. We aren't allowed to use it anymore."

I thought I understood. "Because cyanide is poison?"

Liko nodded as he closed my watch back up. "I've always used it for bombing procedures on gold jewelry. If used correctly with hydrogen peroxide, it produces a very shiny finish to the pieces. Back when I was in my prime, I bought a lot of secondhand jewelry in all sorts of condition. Of course, they had to be cleaned before I could attempt to sell them, and that was often the best way to go about it."

"Isn't such a procedure dangerous?"

He nodded. "Of course. You have to take precautions. With my eyesight the way it is now, I haven't done it in quite a while. Like I said, we technically aren't supposed to use the stuff anymore and could be fined. I heard about one fellow who gave himself a fatal heart attack a few years ago. He forgot to turn off an overhead fan during the cleaning process and ended up inhaling the stuff."

I shuddered inwardly. "That's awful."

Liko handed the watch over the counter to me. "Here you are, miss. That will be fifteen dollars."

I handed him a twenty. His story had been an interesting one but nothing to do with Randolph's fatal encounter. Still, nagging thoughts continued to peck away at my brain. During my snooping, I had come across a previous reference to a jewelry store somewhere, and tried to remember the source.

Recognition suddenly dawned like a bright light at the end of a tunnel. With horror, I brought a hand to my mouth, and a cold shard of fear settled into the center of my spine as I grabbed the counter in front for support. I couldn't be positive of course, but there was a good chance that Liko had just given me my answer.

"Miss?" Liko waved my change and a receipt at me. "You don't look very well. Is everything okay?"

I forced my head to bob up and down like a puppet's. "Fine," I managed to cough out. "Thanks for your help."

As soon as I was on the path back to town, I glanced

down at my watch. Six twenty. Jeff had undoubtedly left to pick me up already and would be thoroughly pissed, but I didn't care. There was no way I could go to rehearsal now. I drew out my phone and texted him.

I can't make it tonight. Sick. So sorry for the inconvenience.

I still hadn't heard from Keanu but knew that he'd message me when he saw my earlier text, so I didn't bother to send another. I scrolled through my contacts for Detective Ray's number. He'd probably think I was crazy—*the girl at the Loco Moco really has gone loco*—but I had to let him know about my theory. I could almost picture the good detective frowning at the phone in distaste, his face as red as the Hawaiian shirt he wore. It didn't matter anymore. I was willing to take that chance.

The call went directly to his voicemail, and I cursed under my breath. How come there was never a cop around when you needed one? Never mind. I'd go back to my apartment and wait for Keanu, tell him my theory, and then maybe we'd drive over to the station together in search of Ray.

My message to Jeff had not exactly been a lie. The conclusion I had drawn *was* enough to make me sick. Still, I prayed that I was wrong. The one thing I hadn't figured out for certain yet was the motive for Randolph's death, but suspected it was money related. I continued to walk on at a furious and brisk pace and barely noticed the sky overhead. It was a glorious hue of red, yellow and orange as the sun began its rapid descent. I usually enjoyed the scent of gardenias coming from a nearby garden but all I could smell now was fear—my own, specifically.

I ran up the steps of the front porch and inserted my key into the lock. I slammed and locked the door behind me then blew out a long breath. I was safe for now. I'd go text Keanu again—no, I'd call him. The meeting had to be winding down, and I really needed to hear his voice. Then I'd call the police station. Maybe someone would be willing to provide me with Ray's home phone number. I couldn't just sit here and wait.

"Ben?" I called. He always came out to greet me. Maybe he was asleep on my bed. I sat down on the couch and noticed that one of the crates with Randolph's items was sitting on top of my coffee table, next to the paper with Wendy's phone number that I had forgotten to take with me. *Strange.* I was certain that I'd placed both crates underneath the table before leaving this morning. As I pulled out my phone, I heard a muffled meow from the bedroom.

"Come here, boy." I absently checked for new messages and waited for Benny to make an appearance. Then I realized that I was not alone in the room.

"Hi, Carrie," a male voice spoke softly.

The hairs on the back of my neck rose at attention, and cold fear washed over me. Swallowing hard, I forced myself to look up. There was a man standing in the doorway of my bedroom, smiling at me. He held Benny in one hand and a sharp kitchen knife in the other.

My theory had been correct, but that didn't exactly make me want to jump for joy. Paralyzed, I continued to sit there in numbed silence.

"I've been waiting for you," he said reproachfully. "It was very rude of you to be so late. What do you have to say for yourself?"

Still in shock, I stared into his angry eyes—eyes that had never given me a reason to be afraid—until now.

"Well?" he asked.

My voice came out in a feeble whisper. "I'm sorry, Jeff."

CHAPTER TWENTY-ONE

"How…how did you get in?" I finally managed to say.

Jeff gripped Benny around the throat with his hand, and the cat hissed. "When I got your text, I was already waiting outside and got suspicious. I rang the bell, but there was no answer. You really shouldn't leave a spare key underneath the mat, Carrie. Some psycho could wander in at any moment."

I never left my key under the mat. Tad had planned to stop over earlier today to take some measurements, but it was obvious now that he'd never made it. In silence, I cursed the hand that fate had dealt me.

Jeff nodded toward the crates. "As soon as I saw Wendy's number and these goodies, I knew you were on to me. I'm surprised she remembered anything from the night of my show. That slut was drunk out of her mind."

I stared at Benny and the knife that was so precariously close to him, then struggled to breathe normally. "Can you put him down, please?"

"Hand me your phone first," Jeff ordered. "Then I'll let the pretty kitty go."

I obediently handed over the phone, and Jeff released his hold on Benny, but not the knife. Benny let out a cry of what might have been relief and scampered off in the direction of my bedroom.

Jeff wasted no time in crushing the phone underneath his foot and gestured at me with the knife. "Sit."

Having no choice, I lowered myself to the couch, and he joined me, placing the blade about an inch away from my throat.

"I don't want to hurt you, Carrie," he said, "but there doesn't seem to be any other way around it. You're too nosy for your own good. It's really going to be the death of you."

He smiled, pleased with his joke, while I cringed and berated myself. If only I had never texted Keanu. He would have come straight to the apartment after his meeting, but instead he'd be waiting for me at the theater around ten o'clock, a place that I would likely never see again. Wait a second. What about the cast? They would be waiting for us and surely be suspicious when we didn't arrive.

"We'll be late for rehearsal." I spoke with optimism and tried to stand.

Jeff reached over and yanked my head back by the hair so that I landed heavily against the cushions of the couch. "Already taken care of," he said. "I sent a text to the stage manager and asked him to get in touch with everyone. I told him we'll reschedule it for tomorrow night. The only difference, of course, is that you won't be there."

Sweat trickled down the small of my back. "You don't want another death on your conscience. Aren't Sean's and Randolph's enough?"

Jeff loosened his grip on my hair, but that didn't matter because the knife was too close to my throat for comfort. Unless help arrived quickly in some shape or form, I was confident he'd cut me up into tiny pieces.

"Well, Carrie." He sounded impressed. "It appears that you might be a better detective than singer. Then again, your singing is about as bad as it can get."

Ouch. Way to hit a girl when she's down.

"How did you make the connection?" Jeff asked, his hot, sour breath against my face, causing nausea to stir in the pit of my stomach. I tried to remain still, afraid any motion might set him off further.

"I don't have all the details," I confessed. "The program from your play said that you were going into the family jewelry business. I wondered if you could have gotten cyanide to poison Randolph from there."

"A very good assumption," he said, "and you'd be correct." Jeff's eyes shifted to the crate on the coffee table. "You were asking Howie an awful lot of questions about Wendy yesterday, so that put me on my guard. Where did you get these crates and the playbill from?"

I didn't answer right away.

He tugged at my hair, and I whimpered in pain. "I asked you a question, Carrie."

I struggled to keep my voice calm. "His daughter gave them to me."

Jeff's eyebrows rose. "I knew he had a kid, but why would she give *you* anything? You're not exactly Nancy Drew, although you seem to think so."

The pain seared through my head. "Please loosen your grip. I'm not going to run, I promise. She…she used to work at the Loco Moco. She has no idea that you are connected. She thinks Belinda is the killer."

Jeff laughed and relaxed his grip. "Good. That's the way it should be. That whore was only interested in his money anyway. I didn't want to kill Randy, but he gave me no choice."

"Why?" I turned my head to look him straight in the face. "Was it because he knew that you killed Sean Tyler?"

Okay, I'd admit. I was winging it a bit with my guess, but why else would he want Randolph dead, except to shut him up? Or perhaps he had been blackmailing Jeff for some reason, but Randolph made more money. What did Jeff have that Randy wanted?

Like a sledgehammer, the truth hit me between the eyeballs, and I remembered what Howie had said the first day we met. "Randolph wanted the Hana Hou, didn't he?"

"Congratulations. You've just won your supersleuth-of-the-year award." Jeff's face brightened. "Maybe I should do a mystery next season. What do you think? Agatha Christie, perhaps? We'll give Rose a white wig, and she can play Miss Marple since you won't be around to star in it. You'll be six feet under by tomorrow."

Not a cheerful thought. "He was blackmailing you?"

"As you know, we all went to school together." Jeff studied the plaque that hung on my wall, *Cats Make a House a Home*. Tad had given it to me as a housewarming gift. "Howie and I were roommates and always got along well. We were also both theater majors. Randy was a communications major and such a prickly little type. Even then he thought he was too good for anyone. Smart, though. He knew how to work the whole media thing back then, before Facebook, Twitter, blogs, and all that other crap. He had a knack for getting people to listen to what he had to say."

I pretended to be interested, but my eyes kept darting around the room while he talked, trying to plan an escape route. Where had Benny wandered off to?

Jeff scowled. "He hung around the theater, writing reviews for the school's newspaper. How that jerk loved to put everyone down. He never cared for me—I guess my disdain for him must have shown. Anyhow, I'd written and directed a musical for my senior project and gave Howie one of the leads so that he could get credit for his own project. Randy offered to get us some extra publicity with a couple of local newspapers, and it was too good to pass up. Of course, he wanted a part in exchange for it. That man always had to have an angle. He was a Kardashian wannabe from that time period—no talent for acting but still wanted all the fame and glory that went with it."

"The girl I chose for the female lead was named Wendy Ritzer," he continued. "She was gorgeous. Oh, we all knew that she was easy, but that was part of the appeal. When she came to the auditions, I couldn't even concentrate. She was like you."

"What?" I managed to squeak out in horror.

He chuckled at my response. "I don't mean that *you're* easy, Carrie. Like you, she had no singing talent."

"Oh, okay." I didn't know if I should be insulted or relieved.

Jeff went on. "On a positive note, her beauty was perfect for the part of Jessica in my show. She had a magnificent stage presence, like you. After the tryouts, she stopped me and hinted that she'd do *anything* for a part. She was a theater major and wanted to use it on her résumé. So I let my hormones decide for me. Typical college boy, right?"

Ew.

"Wendy had a boyfriend," Jeff said. "His name, as you know, was Sean Tyler. I didn't know of him but figured she had to have a guy—or ten. I didn't care—I just wanted to score with her." He paused. "She was my first, if you know what I mean."

Yikes. No more please.

Jeff placed a cold hand at the base of my neck, and I flinched. "The show ran for one night only, and we had a full house. My professor was very pleased, and I knew that Howie and I were both getting A's. We had a cast party backstage afterward to celebrate, and everyone got blitzed." He chuckled. "Finally it was just me and Wendy, and she made good on her promise."

His grip tightened on my throat, and panic, like bile, rose in the back of it. There was no doubt in my mind that Jeff was going to kill me. He had no choice—I knew too much.

"We were in the dressing room, right in the middle of the act—pardon the stage pun—when Sean walked in on us. Of course, he went nuts. Wendy was bombed out of her mind, and when he smacked her across the face, she went lights out. The guy started punching me, and I was no match for him, so I grabbed the first thing I could lay my hands on, which happened to be a baseball bat that we used as one of the props. One whack across the skull, and he was dead." Jeff smiled, as if he found this part mildly amusing.

I tried to appeal to his sane side, but doubted that he had one. "It was self-defense. You should have called the police and explained."

Jeff crossed his legs casually, as if we were having a heart-to-heart chat. *Good.* If he relaxed a little, maybe I stood a better chance of getting away from him.

"I guess I was afraid the police might see right through my facade," Jeff explained as he lowered the knife to my chest. "You see, after he was dead, I realized that I'd enjoyed the kill way too much. I knew Sean wouldn't be my last."

His cold smile sickened me. I glanced over his shoulder, and my eyes focused on the vase of flowers Keanu had brought. Unfortunately, it was too far away to reach. Even if I did manage to get away from Jeff, what about Benny? I couldn't leave him here with this psycho.

The wall clock ticked away in the silent room. Only about ten minutes had passed since Jeff had announced his arrival, but it felt more like ten hours. I had to make a move soon, before it was too late. "What happened after that?" I asked.

"Before I even had a chance to lock the theater doors,

guess who walked backstage?" He didn't wait for my response. "Yep, good old Randy. Seems he'd forgotten something. I figured I was done for, but after I explained what happened, to my surprise he couldn't have been more helpful. He played lookout while I put Sean's body in my trunk, and we carried Wendy outside. I hoped that she'd black the whole thing out. When I ran into her a couple of days later, she acted like nothing had happened, so I figured that was a good sign. After Randy and I took off with Sean's body, I dug a grave in the middle of the night, off a nearby bike trail, while Randy played lookout. I thanked him profusely for his help and told him if he ever needed something, just say the word."

"Guess he said the word, huh?" I managed to choke out.

Jeff shook his head in disgust. "I should have known. At first it wasn't a big deal. I'd get a note that simply said *Word* with an amount printed next to it. Over time, he's gotten worse. Last year when he found out through Howie that I wanted investors, he told me he'd take a fifty percent share of the theater, at no cost to him, of course."

The tip of the knife came to rest underneath my chin, and I didn't dare breathe. Benny appeared in the doorway of my bedroom and yawned as he watched us. *Go away, Ben. Go away.*

"It was never going to end." Jeff's voice was quiet as his eyes fixed on Benny. "I went to see good old Randy the other morning and told him I was thinking about selling the theater. I have an offer on the table that's pretty good. He demanded half the profits if I sold. That's when I knew that I had to get rid of him. I still had some cyanide powder from the family jewelry store. After we shut down a few years ago, I figured it might come in handy someday. Turns out I was right."

Sweat broke out in a river on my forehead. "Did you know I was going to his room that morning with the food?"

He had his face in front of mine now, forcing me to look directly at him. He pressed the blade into my chin until the sharp tip connected with my skin, and I whimpered, seeing nothing but his eyes—a never-ending pool of darkness. "Not *you* in particular. When Randy told me the Loco Moco was bringing us breakfast and you knocked on the door, I excused myself to go to the bathroom. Imagine my surprise when I heard your voice. I already knew what I had to do so it was imperative no one else find me there. Guess you have a real talent for being in the wrong place at the wrong time, Carrie."

There was no doubt about that.

Jeff moved the knife away and squeezed my neck tightly with his other hand, forcing me to gasp for breath. "Of course, when Randy said the coffee was terrible, that was the opportunity I'd been looking for. I knew you'd be coming back, and now you had a motive. The devoted young girl who would do anything for her boyfriend and his family owned business."

Stars were starting to dance before my eyes. "Please," I croaked. "Please don't."

Jeff continued, as if he hadn't heard me. "Right after you left, his cell rang, and he went on the balcony to take the call. That was all the time I needed. I dumped the powder in his coffee cup, and when he came back in, I asked him what was so bad about the coffee. To illustrate the point, he took another sip and then proceeded to give me the lengthy boring details about his beloved Kona coffee. As he started to have spasms, I wiped down a few things I had touched in the room and even remembered to grab my mimosa glass on the way out. It all worked like a charm."

Benny meowed, and Jeff looked over at him. It was the split second I needed for my fingernails to make contact with Jeff's cheek. Jeff let out a howl, and the knife slipped from his grasp. In a fit of rage, he smacked me across the face so hard that I almost blacked out. Before I could move, he pushed me down onto the couch, the weight of his body pressing mine into the cushions as he squeezed my neck tightly between both of his hands.

"Goodbye, Carrie," he whispered. "The curtain is about to go down on your life."

As we struggled, I was dimly aware of orange and white fur as it flew through the air. Benny landed on Jeff's shoulder and clawed him in the face. Jeff screamed and released his hold on me. He reached for Benny while I gulped some much-needed air. The cat hissed at Jeff as he caught him by his hind legs.

At that moment, there was a knock on my front door. "Carrie?" Keanu's worried voice drifted in from the outside.

"No!" I screamed and reached over the arm of the couch to grab the vase, which I wasted no time in bringing down on Jeff's head. He dropped Benny and toppled forward onto my glass coffee table, breaking it in half during the process. He lay on the floor among shards of glass, motionless.

The sound of someone kicking at the front door could be heard. It flew open, and Keanu rushed in. On his way toward me, he stopped for a brief moment when he spotted the body lying there. I stepped over Jeff and ran into Keanu's arms. Benny was now perched on the arm of the couch, contentedly cleaning himself, as if nothing had happened.

"Oh my God." Keanu held me tightly against him. "Are you okay? Did he try to attack you?"

"He tried to kill me. He's the one…killed…Randolph." I wasn't making much sense, but my voice shook so badly that I couldn't control it.

Keanu held me firmly around the waist with one hand as he reached into his pocket with the other for his cell and immediately pressed 9-1-1. "Yes, please send an ambulance to 54 Hani Drive, Apartment 1B. We need police assistance too. A man just tried to kill my girlfriend."

I looked down at Jeff, who still wasn't moving, and laid my head against Keanu's chest until my breathing returned to normal.

He kissed my hair. "Don't worry. He's not going anywhere anytime soon. You got him good, baby." He said something else to the operator and then disconnected the call.

I pressed my face into him, determined not to cry. "How did you know to come here?"

"What do you mean? We had a date, remember?"

I looked up at him, surprised. "Yes, but I sent you a text earlier this afternoon, saying that Jeff wanted to have rehearsal tonight. He came to pick me up and found my key under the mat, so he let himself in. He saw the crates and Wendy's number and suspected that I was on to him."

He pressed his lips against my forehead. "I never saw it. When I got out of the meeting, I had about twenty texts from my father and several vendors. I must have missed yours."

For once Terry had come through on my behalf. "I'll

have to thank your father personally for harassing you so much."

Keanu kept the knife aimed at Jeff's nonmoving body. "Get something to tie his hands up with," he said. "I don't want to take any chances if he comes around before the police get here."

I ran into my bedroom and started to dump items out of my dresser until I found a scarf I'd worn during frigid Vermont winters. I went back to the living room and showed Keanu.

He nodded approval and handed the knife to me. "It's better than nothing." He dropped down next to Jeff's body. "I'll make it as tight as I can."

Once Jeff's hands had been secured, we sat down at the kitchen table next to each other while Keanu kept a sharp eye on Jeff and held the knife firmly in his hand.

"When I heard you scream, I was never so scared in my entire life." He examined my neck and face then glared over at Jeff in obvious contempt. "You've got bruises all over and a black eye. How the hell did you manage to get away from him?"

I turned and pointed at Benny, who was curled up on the arm of the couch, snoozing away. "My new hero."

Keanu looked from Benny to me and grinned. "Well, I'll be damned."

CHAPTER TWENTY-TWO

———

Two weeks later

"Can I help you find something?"

The cheery female voice startled me out of my thoughts. A saleswoman from the Happy Hula Dress Shop was standing next to me, waiting for my response. When our eyes met, we both smiled in recognition.

"Hi, Carrie, how are you?"

I drew my eyebrows together. "Kallie, right?" She'd been in the Loco Moco several times and was always friendly, so I hoped I hadn't botched her name. At that moment, my mind was so preoccupied that I was lucky enough to remember my own.

"Close. It's Kaley. I'm the manager here."

She was pretty, a couple of inches taller than me, and most likely a few years older as well. Kaley's dark hair was almost as long as mine, her pale complexion striking against the red shirt that she wore.

I held up the cobalt silk blouse and knee-length white skirt for her to examine. "What do you think?"

She nodded in approval. "Those will look great together. Are you going on a job interview?"

Heat crept into my cheeks, and I hesitated, afraid to come off sounding like some sort of a braggart. "Sort of. I'm going to Hollywood for a screen test."

Kaley's brown eyes widened. "Wow, that's fantastic. Congratulations! When do you leave?"

"This afternoon. Nothing like waiting until the last minute, huh?" I'd been putting the shopping off until I had a little more money saved up.

She gave me a thumbs-up. "Hey, you've got this. The

dressing room is in the back, if you'd like to try them on."

"I guess I'd better, thanks." I made my way to the rear of the open-floored shop, marveling at the attractive display of bathing suits, towels, and colorful sandals that adorned the walls. It was a treat for me to go clothes shopping because—one, I didn't have any extra money to spare, and two, I never had the time, which explained why I was doing it on the day I was supposed to be leaving Aloha Lagoon.

Vivian, my personal Hollywood gossip expert, had been the one to suggest that I buy a new outfit for my screen test. "Blue," she'd urged. "Make sure that the blouse or dress that you wear is blue. I hear that's the most desired color for screen tests. It represents positive energy." She winked. "What a coincidence that it happens to be the color of your hottie's eyes too."

This sounded plausible enough to me. Besides, I had no other information to go on. I wished that I could be as positive as everyone else was about the trip. A tiny part of me still hoped that Howie would call and say it was all off—the picture would not be made, that there was no money, anything. The entire idea of going to California by myself was nerve wracking enough. When I'd first arrived in Hawaii a few months ago, Brad had been waiting for me, and that had helped. Still, he was living proof now that sometimes it was better to be alone for the right reasons than with someone for the wrong ones.

I quickly slipped off my jeans and T-shirt and tried the outfit on, studying myself critically in the full-length mirror. I had to admit the color of the blouse was vibrant and worked well with my dusky skin tone. There was no time to waste, since I was meeting Keanu and everyone else for a quick goodbye lunch at the Loco Moco in a few minutes.

Terry and Ava had graciously offered to close the restaurant until after lunch so that my fellow employees—and Tad—could all wish me well on my journey. Terry hadn't said much to me in the past two weeks but did thank me for my help in the investigation. He'd also assured me that my job would be waiting for me whenever I returned to Kauai. They'd left for Arizona yesterday, and because of their hectic schedules, we still hadn't had that family dinner yet, which was just fine with me.

I put the skirt and blouse back on their hangers and

wished I'd brought Keanu with me to get his thoughts. Then again, he always said everything looked great on me, which wasn't much help, even though it did do wonders for my self-image.

He'd been right, of course. If I didn't go to California, I would always wonder about what could have been. I had to do this, as much for myself as for our relationship, but that didn't make the decision any easier. After the party, Keanu would drive me to the airport so I could catch my four o'clock flight.

Kaley's voice sounded from the other side of the door. "How'd you make out, Carrie?"

"All set, thanks." Then I looked at the price tags and froze. *Holy cow.* Sure, the blouse was Anne Klein, but it was more than I had imagined. Even with the ten percent discount Aloha Lagoon employees received, there was no way I could justify spending this much money on myself. I had to be extra careful with my cash flow for the next few weeks—until I knew exactly where things stood.

I opened the dressing room door slowly and expected to find Kaley standing there, but she was up front behind the register, in the middle of a phone conversation. She caught sight of me, spoke into the cell again, and then ended the call.

I had hoped to slip the items back onto the rack without being noticed and then casually wave good-bye on my way out the door. No such luck. Kaley was headed toward me, a broad smile on her face. *Great.*

"Well, what do you think? Did you like the outfit?"

"Yes," I said honestly. "It looked great."

Kaley beamed. "Wonderful." She held out her hands for the items. "Shall I take these to the register for you?"

"Um," I hedged. "I really would like to buy them, but they're a little out of my league price wise."

She appeared unconcerned by my comment. "But you like them, right?"

"Yes." I wondered where she was going with this.

"Good. It's settled then." Kaley took the garments and walked toward the register. "Was there anything else you wanted?"

What the heck? "Kaley." I counted to five, an attempt to

control my annoyance. "I just said that I can't afford them."

Kaley laughed in response. "No worries, Carrie. They've already been paid for. The...uh, person who did the good deed said that they wanted to remain anonymous but that you were to buy anything your heart desired. There's no charge on your end."

My jaw dropped. "Who in the world—" A warm tingle ran through me. Of course, I knew who was responsible. There was only one person who would go to such lengths for me. Keanu was generous to a fault with his heart and wallet. I still marveled at how I had ever managed to find him.

Kaley was busy placing the garments in a Happy Hula shopping bag. "Are you sure you don't want anything else? This...ahem...person said it was all right if you wanted to buy the entire store out."

Tears started to gather in the back of my eyes, but I managed a smile for the girl. "No thank you, Kaley. I have everything that I could possibly want." I whispered that one blissful word to myself again. "Everything."

* * *

After lunch, Keanu and I walked hand in hand toward his car as Poncho came rushing out of the kitchen door. "*Ho'aloha*! I almost forgot to give this to you."

The three of us stood by the passenger side of the car, and they both waited while I removed the shiny silver wrapping paper. I stared down in awe at a green sea turtle pendant that hung off a gold chain.

Keanu grinned at Poncho. "Good choice."

I fingered the turtle in amazement. "It's beautiful. Is there some type of significance to the charm?"

Poncho gestured for me to turn around and lift my hair so that he could fasten the chain around my neck. "This is called *honu*. It symbolizes good luck, endurance, and long life." He turned me around and admired the necklace for a second before his voice became gruff. "That is my wish for you always, *ho'aloha*. If you have those three things, you will never need anything more."

I was overwhelmed by the thoughtful gesture and, for

the second time today, moved close to tears. In some ways Poncho was the closest thing to a father I'd ever had, and how I envied his little boys. "I'll treasure it always. Thank you."

To my surprise, he placed his arms around me and gave me a quick peck on the forehead. I returned the hug but was blown away by his action because Poncho hated public displays of affection.

Poncho released his hold on me and patted my cheek. "We will miss you. Come back soon." His eyes had clouded over, like the sky on an overcast day. He turned and walked quickly back toward the Loco Moco.

The dull ache in my chest started to spread to the rest of my body. Keanu opened the car door for me, and I settled into the passenger seat, determined not to cry.

He got behind the wheel and watched me closely. "You okay, sweetheart?"

I nodded but didn't look at him. If I stared into those incredible eyes I was certain to break down.

My flight was on American Airlines and taking off from Lihue Airport. I would change planes in Phoenix with an hour layover and then go on to Burbank from there. Howie would have one of his assistants meet me at the airport and then take me to a nearby hotel. I was even being chauffeured to the studio for my screen test the following day. If they decided that they wanted me for the movie, we would then discuss contract details and more permanent living arrangements.

Tad had suggested that I start hunting for an agent, but I thought it unnecessary. I had no plans to stay in California long term. My life was in Hawaii now. It was home—a word I'd never known the true meaning of before, and I belonged there.

Howie had invited me to join him for dinner tomorrow night after the test so we could talk. It seemed that he was going to an awful lot of trouble for my sake. Perhaps in an odd way Jeff's arrest had something to do with it. Howie had told me— after the initial shock wore off—how grateful he was to me for discovering the truth. He confessed that he had never suspected Jeff was capable of murder. To be honest, neither had I. The theater would continue with productions once a new director and owner had been found.

Jeff had cooperated with the police and even led them to the place where Sean Tyler's body was buried on a bike trail adjacent to the college campus. Dental records had proven the body belonged to him, and his family had been notified. The other day, Vivian had given me the scoop on Randolph's will.

"Look at this." Vivian had pointed eagerly to the latest issue of *People* she'd been reading. "Can you believe that Randolph made a new will a few months ago and left everything to Coral? Guess the man had a conscience after all."

You think you know a person…

"I have something for you," Keanu announced when we got out of the car. He went to the trunk to remove my luggage and pulled out a purple laptop bag. "It was tough to find this color, but I know it's your favorite."

I stared at him in shock. "Oh no, you didn't."

He placed the bag over my shoulder. "But of course I did."

I bit into my lower lip. "Keanu, I can't take this. And for the record, I figured out who my fairy godmother was at the dress shop. Thank you for being so good to me."

Keanu brushed a strand of hair away from my face. "This laptop isn't just for you. It's a present for me too. Now we can skype every day." He grinned and flashed his dimple. "You won't have time to miss me if you see me every day."

"I already miss you." It was the truth. I watched his strong jaw tighten and the well-defined features focus on me while the pain started to swell inside my chest.

He put a finger on my lips. "I feel the same way. Come on, sweetheart. We need to go find your plane."

We checked my bags and then slowly walked toward security with our hands entwined. After we reached that point, I'd be forced to separate from him. There wasn't much of a line, so we lingered in a corner for a few minutes and indulged in a few of those public displays of affection that Poncho hated so much. I wrapped my arms around his waist, as he stroked my cheek softly.

"I don't want to go." I sounded like a five-year-old but didn't care. I'd waited twenty-five years for someone to love me. Right now three months away from this man seemed like an eternity.

Keanu shushed me with a kiss. "This is your dream. I want you to go, and deep down, you want it too. Remember that nothing is going to keep us apart for very long. You'll come back to me—I'm sure of that. If I thought there was a chance you wouldn't—" His voice grew tight and hoarse. "Then I'd never let go."

The tears rolled down my cheeks, and Keanu wiped them away with his thumb. "This is the right thing to do," he said. "Remember that line in *Little Women* that you say to Jo when you know you're dying?"

All too well. "Promise me that you won't be sad," I quoted.

"That's right," he whispered. "I don't want you to ever be sad. This is only for a few months out of the rest of our lives. Then with any luck, we'll be together for a long time after that. Okay?"

I wasn't sure what exactly he was implying, but regardless, it sounded wonderful to my hopeful ears. "Okay. I love you. Bye."

"Don't say goodbye." His eyes brimmed with moisture. "Tell me that you'll see me soon."

His image grew cloudy through my tears, but I managed a smile for him. "See you soon, Watson."

He released my hand, and I presented my ticket to the airport employee. I placed my laptop, purse, and shoes on the conveyer belt to be X-rayed and then walked through the full body scanner. Fortunately, I didn't set it off, since I had cut things close time-wise.

After I made my way through the machine and had placed my sneakers back on, I turned and looked back one last time at Keanu. He smiled and gave me a thumbs-up. Then I rounded the corner, and he disappeared from my sight.

So much for my act of bravery. Tears started to sting the backs of my eyes, and I quickly brushed them away as I boarded the plane and found my assigned seat next to a window. I kept staring at the side of the airport, as if I expected to see him jump out a door at any moment. It was silly, but I couldn't help myself. Then I closed my eyes and reminded myself that I was doing the right thing.

To keep myself occupied, I decided to check out my new laptop. As I waited for the screen to load, I marveled at Keanu's generosity again. He planned to fly out in two weeks, after his parents returned to Kauai. Keanu would also visit a couple of grocery stores along the way. He'd already bought his ticket, so this gave me something to look forward to. I exhaled a long, deep breath. Everything was going to be fine.

The screensaver Keanu had loaded was enough to make the waterworks start again. It was a selfie we'd taken last week of the both of us with Benny in my arms. Benny was staring directly at the camera, his eyes wide with curiosity, and such a comical expression on his face that I laughed every time I saw the picture. Now I knew why Keanu had chosen it.

Don't be sad. It was impossible to feel anything but joy when I looked at this picture.

I owed a lot to that furry feline—my life for one. It had been difficult to leave him this morning, and somehow he must have sensed that I was going away, because he'd acted strange, even hiding under the bed when I'd asked for one last hug. He was in good hands with Tad, and Keanu had promised to stop and see him as well.

"Excuse me."

Startled, I looked up. An elderly woman with short, white curly hair addressed me, a broad smile on her narrow face. She gestured at the laptop bag that I'd placed on the seat next to me. "I believe that's my seat, dear."

"Oh, sorry about that." I removed the bag. "I wasn't thinking."

She sat down and drew the seat belt across her tiny frame. "I'm Leslie." She extended a tiny hand covered in liver spots, with transparent blue veins. "I came to the island to visit my son, but I live in Arizona."

"Carrie. I live in Kauai, but I'm on my way to California. Nice to meet you."

Her eyes traveled to my laptop and suddenly widened. "Likewise. Oh my. Is that your husband?"

My cheeks warmed. "Boyfriend."

She nodded in approval. "He's a hot one. Looks like a

keeper to me."

"He is." I bit into my lower lip to keep from laughing.

"How come he's not with you?" Leslie wanted to know.

I didn't find her questions intrusive in the least and welcomed the conversation. I'd never known either one of my grandmothers and had always craved that special bond. "I'm going to Hollywood for a screen test, and he has commitments here. We won't be separated for very long."

She studied me carefully. "Well, you're certainly pretty enough for Hollywood. You remind me of my youngest granddaughter. She's a singer—even cut a record," Leslie said proudly.

"That's fantastic." I stared wistfully at the screen saver, wishing Keanu was sitting here too.

Leslie continued to watch me and must have guessed what was running through my head. "I'll bet he's missing you too. He must really love you if he's willing to let you go like this."

My heart fluttered at the words. "Yes. I'm very lucky."

She rested the back of her head against the seat and closed her eyes. "You'll be back with him before you know it, honey, so make the most of it while you can. Grab that brass ring because there are no guarantees in this life that you'll ever get another one. A man that truly loves you will wait—mark my words. Your relationship will be stronger afterwards too."

"You sound as if you speak from experience."

Leslie opened one eye and winked. "Maybe I do."

I stared out the window at the lush greenery of the island. Once again I thanked my lucky stars that had brought me to tropical paradise. Keanu had once mentioned that fate had brought me here, not Brad, and I didn't doubt it for a second.

The plane started to taxi down the runway, and I recalled how it had felt when I arrived in Hawaii for the first time a few months ago. I'd been nervous but excited and filled with anticipation. The same thing was true now. Leslie was right—I needed to make the most of the experience while it lasted. Keanu had known this from the beginning, as well as the fact that our relationship would make it through just fine.

As the plane gathered height in the air, I glanced down at

Kauai—my home—for one last time. "I'll be back soon." I whispered the words softly to the window so that Leslie didn't hear. "Nothing will stop me."

RECIPES

Loco Moco

Ingredients:
Cooking spray
1 pound ground beef chuck
1 cup sliced onion
½ cup water (to enhance the flavor, use chicken broth in place of water)
1 12-ounce jar brown gravy
4 eggs
4 cups cooked rice
Prepare a large skillet with cooking spray, and heat over medium heat. Divide the ground chuck into 4 equal portions and form into patties. Fry the patties in the skillet until they begin to firm and are hot and slightly pink in the center, about 6 minutes per side. Remove patties to a plate, retaining drippings in the skillet. Stir onion and water into the reserved drippings. Reduce heat to low, and cook until the onions are slightly softened, about 5 minutes. Pour gravy over the onion mixture, and stir. Cook until the gravy is hot, about 5 minutes. Gently lay patties in the gravy, then simmer until reheated through. While the patties simmer in gravy, prepare a separate skillet with cooking spray, and heat over medium heat. Fry eggs in the hot skillet until the white is opaque but the yolk remains runny, about 2 to 3 minutes. Divide the rice between 4 plates. Top each rice portion with a beef patty, and top the patties each with an egg. Pour gravy equally over each portion. Makes four servings.

Aloha Mix-Up Cookies

Ingredients:
1 cup unsalted butter, room temperature
1 cup granulated sugar
1 cup light brown sugar, packed
2 eggs, room temperature
2 tsp vanilla extract
3 cups (14.4 ounces) all-purpose flour
½ tsp baking soda
1 tsp sea salt

Mix-ins (use as much or as little as you wish)
¾ cup white chocolate chips
1/2 cup macadamia nuts, coarsely chopped
½ cup dried pineapple, chopped
½ cup sweetened flaked coconut
Don't preheat the oven first, as the dough needs to chill for a minimum of 30 minutes.
In a medium bowl, whisk together all-purpose flour, salt, and baking soda. Set aside. Using a stand mixer or a large bowl with an electric mixer, cream together the butter with the granulated sugar and brown sugar on medium speed until fluffy, about 2 minutes. Add the eggs, one at a time, beating well after each addition. Stir in the vanilla extract. Add the flour all at once, and pulse the mixer to keep flour from flying. Once mostly combined, increase speed, and mix until flour is completely incorporated. Resist the urge to overmix. Note: If using a hand-held electric mixer, you will need to add the flour in increments.
Mix-ins: You can stir the white chocolate chips, macadamia nuts, dried pineapple, and coconut into the dough or mix and match. You can create several combinations of cookies by dividing the dough between four bowls and mixing in some of the white chocolate chips with macadamia nuts into one, pineapple and coconut into another, pineapple and macadamia nuts in the third, and using all four mix-in ingredients in the last portion. Or make up your own combinations.

Place the bowls of dough in the refrigerator, and allow to chill for at least 30 minutes and up to 2 days. When ready to bake, preheat oven to 350 degrees Fahrenheit. Line a baking sheet with parchment paper and scoop tablespoon-sized rounds of dough onto the sheet. Bake 10–12 minutes or until the bottom of the cookie starts turning lightly golden. Rotate baking sheet halfway through baking. Allow cookies to rest on the baking sheet for 3 minutes before transferring to a cooling rack. Cool completely before storing in an airtight container.

Makes 6 dozen cookies, depending on size. Tip: If you refrigerate the dough longer than 30 minutes, allow the dough to sit at room temperature for 10 minutes to making scooping easier.

Ahi Tuna

Ingredients
1 pound sushi-grade ahi tuna, cubed
2 tbsp soy sauce
1 tsp rice wine vinegar
2 tsp orange juice
2 tsp toasted sesame oil
1 tsp grated fresh ginger
¼ cup sweet onion, thinly sliced
2 green onions thinly sliced, green parts only
1 tsp sesame seeds (white or black)
½ tsp red pepper flakes, optional for spicy poke
Whisk together soy sauce, rice wine vinegar, orange juice, toasted sesame oil, fresh ginger, and red pepper flakes if using. Place cubed ahi, sweet onion, and green onion in a serving bowl. Drizzle the soy sauce mixture over the ahi and gently toss to coat. If not consuming immediately, refrigerate. Sprinkle with sesame seeds, and stir to mix in just before serving.
Serve the ahi poke with warm steamed rice, fresh mango, avocado, pickled ginger, and seaweed salad, allowing diners to create their own poke bowls. Do not allow leftovers to sit at room temperature. Refrigerate immediately and eat within two days.
Options for serving: steamed white rice, cubed fresh avocado, cubed fresh mango, and pickled ginger seaweed salad.

Pineapple Cookies

Ingredients
1 ½ cup of sugar
2 eggs
2 cups crushed pineapple, fresh or canned, strained (reserve 3 tbsp. of the juice for glaze)
3 cups flour
1 tsp baking soda
1 tsp vanilla
Pinch of salt
1 to 1 ½ cup confectioner's sugar (for glaze)
½ cup butter

Preheat oven to 350 degrees Fahrenheit. Cream together sugar, eggs, butter, and vanilla. Add pineapple and stir well. Add flour, baking soda, and salt, stir well again. Drop cookies by spoonful onto waxed paper. Cool for ten minutes. If glaze for cookies is desired, combine the reserved pineapple juice and confectioner's sugar to a consistency. Drizzle over cooled cookies. Makes about three dozen.

ABOUT THE AUTHOR

USA Today bestselling author Catherine Bruns lives in Upstate New York with a male dominated household that consists of her very patient husband, three sons, and assorted cats and dogs. She has wanted to be a writer since the age of eight when she wrote her own version of Cinderella (fortunately Disney never sued). Catherine holds a B.A. in English and is a member of Mystery Writers of America and Sisters in Crime.

To learn more about Catherine Bruns, visit her online at:
http://www.catherinebruns.net

Visit the official

website!

Trouble in paradise...
Welcome to Aloha Lagoon, one of Hawaii's hidden treasures. A little bit of tropical paradise nestled along the coast of Kauai, this resort town boasts luxurious accommodation, friendly island atmosphere...and only a slightly higher than normal murder rate. While mysterious circumstances may be the norm on our corner of the island, we're certain that our staff and Lagoon natives will make your stay in Aloha Lagoon one you will never forget!

www.alohalagoonmysteries.com

If you enjoyed *Death of the Kona Man*, be sure to pick up these other Aloha Lagoon Mysteries!

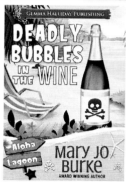